Air in Judgement

Air in Judgement

Written and illustrated by
David Schmidt

Brule, Wisconsin

AIR IN JUDGEMENT

First Edition

Published by:

Cable Publishing
14090 E Keinenen Rd
Brule, WI 54820

Website: www.cablepublishing.com
E-mail: nan@cablepublishing.com

This is a work of fiction. Any resemblance to actual people,
living or dead, is purely coincidental.

Soft cover: ISBN 13: 978-1-934980-29-3
             ISBN 10: 1-934980-29-3

Library of Congress Control Number: 2009942870

Printed in the United States of America

This book is dedicated to my aunt Renny who was the guide to my spirit of creativity as a child and an inspiration along life's path.
– DS

ORIGIN

A butterfly gently fluttered over a peaceful meadow and landed on a small sapling. Its bright orange and yellow wings silently flapped as it tried to keep its balance on the thin twig.

Chirps from dozens of birds and the occasional chatter of insects were the only sounds that radiated from the quiet valley. A soft wind gingerly blew against the trees and mildly tossed their leaves about. The tall grasses and wildflowers on the forest floor slowly swayed back and forth like waves on the shore of a calm lake.

Suddenly, two small, furry animals burst from the tree line and tumbled in a heap out into the sun.

"Gotcha!" exclaimed the smaller of the two, a gray wolf pup. "Ya can't hide from me! I've got natural hunting and tracking skills!"

"Oh, gimme a break, Mesquite," said the other round ball of fur, a grizzly bear cub. "I stopped playing hide-and-seek when I came across those raspberry bushes. I was on a l-l-lunch break," he stuttered. The little bear liked to eat.

"Sequoia, you lost fair and square and now you're gonna have to find me!" Mesquite quipped.

"I'm tired of this game. Let's g-g-go mess with Aspen instead," the little grizzly offered.

"Okay, loser, since you can't win anyway." Mesquite snipped. "I think she's up on the bluffs. My mom said she saw her this morning."

The two friends started off across the valley toward a large, rocky summit overlooking the meadow.

"Why does she always want to g-g-go up there?" Sequoia asked.

"She likes to pretend she's flying since she's not very good at it," Mesquite said. "Her mom and dad get her up there and show her that peregrine falcons are good flyers and she should be soaring with them by now."

"M-m-maybe she's really not a peregrine falcon at all," Sequoia joked. "Maybe she's a chicken!"

Mesquite burst out laughing at the little bear's comment as they plowed headlong through the long grasses toward the path that led up the cliff.

After the duo had plodded along for nearly an hour, they finally neared the top of the bluff. They could see their little friend, Aspen, out on the edge of a craggy rock. She had her eyes closed and was holding her wings out, pretending to be soaring above the valley. The wind was blowing against her, rustling her feathers

as though she was actually flying.

Mesquite hunkered down so she wouldn't see him. "Hey, Sequoia," he whispered to his friend, "let's sneak up on her and scare her off the cliff! We'll teach her to fly, all right!"

"Not me. You g-g-go ahead. She'll tell her mom and her mom will tell my mom and I'll g-g-get grounded until hibernation time!" the bear replied.

"Fine. I'm not scared. You just sit back and watch an alpha-male wolf in action!" Mesquite said confidently.

He turned away from Sequoia and peered quietly over some blades of grass. He got ready to pounce.

Whack!

Without warning, a small white and blue wing slapped Mesquite across the face and he fell over backward, holding his nose with his front paws.

"Thought you could sneak up on me, huh?" Aspen said proudly, as she tucked her wing back alongside her body. "I heard you a mile away, you idiot!"

"It was his idea!" Mesquite said, pointing his paw at Sequoia.

"Oh, really!" Aspen said, glaring at the bear cub.

"N-n-no it wasn't!" Sequoia stammered. "It wasn't me. He's lying! Mesquite, I'm gonna kick your —"

Suddenly, the roar of a private jet cut off the adolescent grizzly. It cruised low and fast and blasted by

them with a horrendous shudder. It was a stealthy, high-tech aircraft — shiny black in color, but with bright red symbols on the sides. It was making a high-speed getaway back to its home base after a secret and successful mission of arson.

"What was that?!" Aspen exclaimed. "How rude!"

The three friends shook the dust off and looked in the direction of the jet. It was already out of sight.

Sequoia stuck his nose up and smelled the air in the jet's wake. "Do you smell smoke?" he asked.

Mesquite and Aspen joined their friend in sniffing the air. The normally fresh, clean air of the valley was mixing heavily with the scent of burning wood.

"You're right," Mesquite said. "The forest is on fire!"

The trio bounded over to the other side of the bluff from where the jet had first appeared for a better look at the valley below.

What they saw shocked them. A wild, ferocious fire was rapidly consuming the forest below. Orange and red flames ripped at the trees and grasses as clouds of thick, grayish-black smoke poured upward into the sky. The fire was accelerating and encircling the entire valley. It looked as though it would consume everything.

"We gotta get home!" the three friends exclaimed at practically the same time.

Aspen leaped off the cliff, flapping her little wings

fiercely as she struggled to fly. "I'll check the way!" she yelled to the wolf and bear younglings as they hustled down the path to the valley below.

The artificially inspired fire raged and very quickly devoured everything in its path. It swarmed over the valley like a fiery flood.

In a panic, Mesquite and Sequoia scrambled down the trail. Terrified, they were trying to get back to their dens where their families were surely waiting for them. As they rounded a corner near the end of the trail, they encountered Aspen on a tree limb overlooking the path.

"We can't go this way!" she shouted as she tried to catch her breath. Her wings were tired from flying just a short distance. "We have to go around to the east," she said, pointing with her wing. "If we can get over the river, we can catch up with our families from the other side. I won't be able to fly much more. We have to hurry!"

The boys nodded and headed off through the brush and around the hillside. It was slow going since there was no trail and neither of them had ever gone that way before. They were all scared.

The sky was blackening and all the smoke was blotting out the sun. It started to look like dusk even though it was a sunny afternoon. Everything had a dark orange, hazy look to it. The hoarse rumbling sounds

of the fire made it hard to hear. The swirling winds generated by the flames carried an amazing amount of gray ash, making it look almost as if it were snowing.

The three animals finally got to the far side of the hill only to find the valley that faced them already submitting to the power of the flames.

"We've got to go back!" Mesquite shouted, and he started to turn around.

The fire was overrunning the forest behind them. Trees, still aflame, toppled in the forest and crashed to the ground. The fire had surrounded them.

"There's only one way out!" Sequoia yelled above the noise and confusion. "We have to jump in the river and let it carry us out of here! Aspen, you can ride on me down the stream — I know you can't swim."

"Let's do it!" Mesquite plunged into the river and was immediately swept away by its torrent. Sequoia followed him in without hesitating. Aspen flew down and landed on the cub's back as Sequoia frantically tried to paddle for control.

The river rushed them along through the burning forest. They passed safely through intense patches of heat and thick black smoke. Flames leaped out from all directions but never touched the hapless trio as they whirled about in the rushing waters. Burning embers fell about them, extinguishing with a loud hiss as they hit the water.

After a while, the burning forest slowly disappeared behind them. The air grew cleaner and the sky was clearer as the river snaked its way down through a ravine.

The river was running faster and faster, and they soon found themselves at risk of being drowned instead of burned alive.

Mesquite and Sequoia were almost exhausted from swimming so hard. Aspen was doing all she could to hang on. Her little talons gripped the fur of her young grizzly friend as tightly as possible.

A short distance ahead, Mesquite could see the river becoming very rough, with jutting boulders and dangerous fast-moving water. The drenched little wolf pup turned to his friends splashing violently behind him.

"We've got to get out of the river!" he shouted. "There's a dead tree up ahead hanging over the water. Grab onto it and pull yourselves out!"

The trio slammed into the fallen tree but managed to hang on with their claws as the rushing river pulled at them. Aspen had just enough energy left to fly onto the log and she shouted desperately for her friends to get out of the river.

Mesquite managed to get out first and, after getting a firm grip, he bent over and grabbed onto Sequoia with his teeth. He tugged and tugged until the soaked bear got a foothold on a branch and hoisted himself out of the raging waters.

They stumbled off the tree and collapsed onto a thin strip of ground. Panting heavily and trying to catch their breath, they could see that they were at the base of a rocky wall next to the river.

After a few minutes of lying there, trying to regain their strength, they were startled by a cry for help from the river. They bolted upright and peered over the riverbank. Swimming frantically just upstream, a small, lanky animal was helplessly heading for the rapids.

"W-w-we got to save her!" Sequoia bellowed. He sprang on the fallen tree and held his paw down into the water to try to rescue the distressed creature caught in the river's current.

As she came by, she latched onto the grizzly cub's thick paw. Sequoia lifted her easily out of the water and onto the relative safety of the tree limb. The wiry animal shook the water off herself and scampered to solid ground. The others could now clearly see that she was a young black-footed ferret.

"Oh, thank you, thank you. You saved my life!" she said to Sequoia as he joined them on the riverbank. "My name is Juniper. What's yours?"

The grizzly bear, gray wolf and peregrine falcon young-lings introduced themselves to their new friend as wisps of smoke and ash swirled all around. The fire was darkening the sky above them. It was getting closer.

"C'mon," Mesquite said. "We've gotta keep moving. The wind's blowing the fire this way. We'll have to walk from here."

The exhausted quartet got to their feet and headed away from the approaching wildfire. The raging river was to one side of them, the rocky cliff to the other, and the fire was quickly approaching from the rear.

They didn't get more than a few dozen steps before their thin pathway stopped abruptly at the top of a sheer drop-off to the rapids below.

Aspen flew up onto Sequoia's shoulders to peer over the edge. "End of the road, guys," she said. "What are we going to do now?"

The animals looked around and at each other. Things had gotten pretty grim.

Just then, they heard a voice from the craggy rock face above. "Up here! Climb up! You'll be safe up here!" It was a badger cub calling down to them from a ledge.

The animals were relieved, but knew they couldn't scale the rocks to get to him.

"How do we get up there? It's too steep!" Juniper shouted up to him as she stood up on her back feet.

"There's sort of a path back that way a bit," the badger yelled down to them while pointing with his paw. "It's not easy, but you should be able to make it. You better hurry!"

The group wasted no time and a few minutes later, after clambering up the rocks, they came face to face with the little badger high above the river.

"C'mon," their rescuer said. "There's a cave back this way. We'll be safe there."

"Thanks, friend," Sequoia said. "What's y-y-your name?"

"Cedar," he said.

"Well, Cedar, I'm Sequoia," the bear said. "This is Aspen, that's Mesquite and she's Juniper."

"That's quite a wildfire," Cedar said as he glanced over his shoulder. "We should all consider ourselves lucky. Like you guys, I barely escaped getting cooked back there. Fortunately, I came across this cave."

The group walked around a large boulder at the mouth of the cave. Cedar led them into the cool, dark opening and along a thin, sandy trail down deep inside the underground cavity. They eventually came to a larger open area where they all could sit and rest. In a few hours, the firestorm should harmlessly pass them by.

It took a moment for all of them to finally relax a little and dwell mournfully on the tragic events of the day. They were orphaned animals now.

Without warning, a man emerged out of the shadows of the cave. It was an elderly tribal chief. He wore a glorious headdress of feathers and beads. His clothes

were made of buckskin, as were the moccasins on his feet. The old chief held a very old and oddly shaped walking stick. He made absolutely no sound when he moved and as he stepped forward, his feet never quite touched the ground. He seemed to be somewhat transparent.

The animals were startled by his presence. They jumped back and gathered tightly together on the other side of the cave.

"Do not be frightened," he said. "This is my home; I am the great chief of the shamans of the tribes of the four winds. You are my guests, and I have been expecting you for a very long time. You have been brought here to be together, for the five of you are truly one."

The badger decided that he had had enough of this stranger and his strange ways. He stepped forward a little and bared his teeth, hoping to scare the ghost-man away.

"I mean you no harm, Cedar," the Native American said. The ancient man could tell that they feared him.

Cedar backed down.

"Oh," the chief said as he chuckled a little. "I see you are shocked that I know your names. I know all of you and, believe it or not, all of you know me — at least in your hearts."

The animals looked at each other, puzzled. This was

truly a day of amazing events.

"We speak the same language, you and I. Your ancestors taught us the ways of nature...the circle of life. They taught us to dance, to sing and to laugh. And they also taught us to fight and survive," the old spirit said. "And, now, it is time to fight again."

The tribal chief sat down, his legs crossed beneath him. He still did not touch the ground; instead he mysteriously hovered several inches above it.

"Gather around me, my brothers and sisters," the Native American said as he spread out his arms. "Much has been taken from you this day...but much is about to be given. You are a family now. Stay together, for you will be the law of the land."

The animals approached the spirit-chief, no longer afraid of him. They sat in a semicircle in front of him and listened intently.

The shaman waved his walking stick across the ground in front of them, and a small, bright-blue flame snaked up from under the sand and stones of the cave floor. It danced and flickered, finally growing into a small, mystical campfire. The flames generated no heat, only a metaphysical, turquoise-colored light that bounced off the cave walls all around them.

"The earth has been dishonored too many times, my friends. She is bountiful, but she can take no more. The

evil that has come over this land must be stopped. You five have been chosen to be her guardians," the elder revealed.

The animals heard ancient Native American drums and chants from invisible people echo throughout the cavern. The sounds grew louder and louder, but the old chief was the only one there with them. The blue-green blaze on the cave floor burned brighter.

"Now reach into the fire, my brothers and sisters. Remove a stone from the enchanted flames," he said.

The animals, eyes open wide in wonderment, hesitantly leaned into the magical blaze and each pulled out a small, flat stone. The strange turquoise fire did not burn at all, but tickled their skin. The five creatures of the forest sat back, looking down at the glowing gems in their grasp.

"Now turn them over, and you will see that each stone is marked with your imprint," said the spirit chief. The animals did as they were told and noticed their footprints had pressed into the rock on the other side.

"These are the source of your power; you must keep them with you at all times," he continued. "It is told that turquoise has healing and protective powers. It promotes spiritual harmony and dispels negative energy and impurity. You have been granted great responsibility and great authority. The spirits of the entire first

nations are behind you, and the fate of mother earth is before you."

The shaman reached into a satchel tied to his belt and pulled out five long, leather cords. He went to each animal, tied a cord to their amulet stones, and placed them around their necks like a pendant. He then stepped back behind the flickering fire and smiled at his animal audience.

"When you are in danger," he said as they looked up at him in amazement, "the amulets will bring the spirits of your animal and native warrior ancestors into your hearts. You will become more powerful than you can imagine. It is your destiny to right the wrongs of the land and bring balance back to the planet. You only have to believe...."

Suddenly, the blue-green fire separated into five distinct flames and shot straight into each animal's amulet. The necklaces glowed brightly with an intense neon-blue color that swirled about the five little animals like a tornado made of pure light.

Then, with one last powerfully brilliant flash, each animal transformed into his or her powerful, noble alter-ego. They raised up on their hind legs, human-like, in a proud, heroic stance with their heads held high and their chests jutting forward.

Mesquite transformed into a large, valiant humanoid

wolf with incredible fighting skills, armed with a long wooden staff with an enchanted spear tip that he could summon at will.

Aspen became a regal falcon-woman, her wings tipped with mystical feathers that she could shoot like missiles with deadly accuracy and power.

Sequoia morphed into a massive, muscular, fully grown man-like grizzly with a huge, unbreakable magical shield grasped in his left arm.

Cedar grew into a stocky, brawny man-sized badger with claws that could carve through steel and tunnel him at incredible speeds behind enemy lines.

Finally, Juniper changed into an ultra-athletic and extremely flexible ferret-woman blessed with super-speed. Whenever she transformed, a leather pack automatically appeared on her back that was filled with small wooden handles that she could magically turn into hatchets with just her touch.

The Natural Forces heroes looked at each other and felt their newly found power course through their superhuman bodies. Together, they felt unstoppable.

Without another word, the shaman chief had disappeared back into the shadows from which he came, bound for his home in the spirit realm.

Their adventures were about to begin and the world would never be the same.

Out of the smog-choked sky over Los Angeles juts a 30-story skyscraper of black steel and mirrored glass. It is a menacing and imposing building, cold and calculated in its design, and it sits far away from the rest of the gigantic city's other superstructures that huddle together in the business district downtown. Instead, the dark monolith that serves as the headquarters for the Axxes Conglomeration is tucked up against the power-producing industrial and electrical complex just outside of the LA skyline. More often than not, the endless clouds of burning coal and steam cloak most of the black tower, hiding it from view.

Clouded in secrecy, the Axxes mega-corporation is guarded by a dense layer of security. Gaining access inside is nearly impossible and only those who have been invited, and carefully checked, gain entry. Dark and vile acts have been – and continue to be – practiced by this company as a necessary means to achieve their objectives.

Nathan Axxes is the President and Chief Executive Officer of the global corporation that bears his name.

He is a ruthless, intimidating man who is driven by greed and fills his overwhelming thirst for power by looting resources from the planet and manipulating others to reap his rewards.

Mr. Axxes, which is how he demands to be called, is wealthy beyond measure. His corporation is international and involved in banking, research, development, manufacturing and especially energy and resource production. The Axxes Conglomeration has operations all across the planet harvesting old-growth rainforests, ripping valuable resources from the earth and devouring fuel and water at massive levels to keep his operations running day and night.

He has invested billions into cutting-edge military-like construction machinery and most of his gigantic labor force is made up of advanced human-like robotic drone workers called Soldierjacks. He prefers them to human counterparts because they work endlessly for no pay with no complaints and they have three times the strength of an ordinary man. With an army of tireless mechanized workers and their brutally effective militaristic construction equipment, the Axxes Conglomeration is without doubt the most damaging force the earth has ever experienced.

On this day, like many others inside the Axxes headquarters, loud rhythmic metallic clacks echo down the

hallways. Those familiar with this sound know full well it harkens the arrival of Doctor Zhao Kaustik, Chief of Research and Advanced Design and head scientist for Axxes. Today, he is on his way to a board meeting with Mr. Axxes to present the results of the Toxic Air Capacitor he has been building for the last several months.

Dr. Kaustik is a frail, older man of Mongolian origin whose body is so infused with the poisons he has developed over the last several decades that he cannot breathe on his own. His skin has turned a greenish-gray color and his hair has fallen out in clumps with just a few random patches of dead, white hair remaining on his pockmarked head.

He is forced to wear thick protective gloves because even his touch can cause sickness in others. Dr. Kaustik exhales deadly gases that, without filtering and processing, would be lethal to any who would inhale them. And so Kaustik designed and built a mobile life-support workstation that follows him wherever he goes. Called SPIDER (Self-Powered Integrated Dependent Existence Robot), this device is a horrific machine of evil manufacture.

Kaustik's gigantic metal SPIDER weighs nearly a ton and stands over seven feet tall. Despite its massive size, Kaustik's robotic assistant moves with grace and extreme quickness. The bright green SPIDER has

six large alloy legs that first bend down, then back up over its body, finally tapering down into sharp tips. These legs flex and move much like an actual insect's legs and allow the SPIDER to fit into much smaller spaces and climb surfaces that would seem impossible.

Its head is made up of advanced, integrated computer systems with a main monitor sitting behind a complex keyboard and an array of buttons on its face. On the SPIDER's back sits a series of canisters, machines and other breathing devices that provide clean air for Dr. Kaustik to breathe, but also convert his deadly exhalations into a thick toxic liquid which the SPIDER can utilize as deadly venom if put into offensive mode.

If set to "Defend and Attack," the SPIDER temporarily releases from its host and turns into an artificially intelligent and very deadly foe. In addition to the processed toxic venom it fires in a compressed stream from a pair of nozzles located where a lower jaw would be if this machine were actually alive, the SPIDER is also armed with an electromagnetic cord fired from its tail.

Mimicking the silk webbing cast from a real spider, this highly charged, incredibly strong cable shoots out from behind Kaustik's mechanical nightmare with extreme accuracy and deadly results. Hooked inside

the body of the man-made arachnid to a high-speed winch, the cable can also reel in whatever it catches in its coils.

When necessary, the mechanical beast also uses its six long legs with laser-sharpened alloy tips to smash, slash or impale targeted enemies. Dr. Kaustik ensures his SPIDER has the most modern battle software loaded at all times and likes to watch it destroy Soldierjacks set against it during training trials.

As Dr. Kaustik headed down the hall, connected by the heavy, black breathing hoses to his giant creepy mechanical SPIDER perfectly in step right behind him, other Axxes employees quickly scurried out of his way. The doctor enjoyed watching others scatter before him, fearful of his power and his trusty mechanical monster.

When he reached the boardroom, Dr. Kaustik raised his hand to knock but was instead summoned inside by a voice from within before he could even make contact with the door.

"Come in, Doctor," Nathan Axxes loudly proclaimed, having heard the click-clack-click-clack sounds from the pointy legs of the SPIDER striking the tiled floor in the hallway as they approached. "I trust you have nothing but good news to report," he added in a lightly veiled threat as the doors parted remotely and his

underling entered the room.

"Most certainly, Mr. Axxes, sir," Dr. Kaustik said through his breathing respirator as he moved toward the front of the room where his boss sat. The polluted scientist laid several packets of his project report on the long boardroom table and turned around to face his SPIDER. With his gloved hands, he typed away quickly on the keyboard mounted to his robotic lung machine to bring up his prepared presentation.

Suddenly, a small projector popped up from a hidden compartment on the face of the SPIDER and the huge mechanical arachnid lowered and positioned itself so as to project the doctor's slideshow onto the massive screen at the front of the conference room.

With the SPIDER hunkered down and the title screen now displayed, the doctor turned again to face Nathan Axxes and his squad of evil executives gathered around the conference table. Axxes grinned and interweaved his long, spindly fingers as he read the title slide, "Project Phoenix. Ready for Testing."

"Gentlemen," the doctor began; his voice gurgled, scratchy and hoarse. "After months of development and implementation, we are ready to test the capacitor. We have selected an ideal site — a large cavern in Arizona in a remote region of the Grand Canyon. The site is nearly impossible to get to, keeping interlopers

away, and has access to the river, which we need to help process the chemicals. The noise from the rushing waters should also help mask the sound the machines produce. The area offers an excellent red clay soil that when dried and pulverized into a fine dust serves as the carrier for the concoction.

"A long projection tube will launch the product into the atmosphere from our location in the cave 1500 meters below the surface," he continued. "The site is on the exact coordinates within our parameters for an easterly jet-stream trajectory. Soldierjack teams were deployed thirteen weeks ago to expand and reinforce the cave walls. Once phase one was complete, we rebuilt the entire capacitor on-site and installed it deep within the cavern, hidden from view. The whole site is protected from prying eyes, wandering hikers and meddling park rangers."

Dr. Kaustik tapped a key on the SPIDER to advance his slideshow presentation as he spoke. Detailed blueprints with the words CLASSIFIED across the top displayed on the screen toward the front of the room. Photos of the cave and Soldierjacks busily working on the installation were intermixed with blueprints, spreadsheets and scientific calculations.

"As you can see by this slide," the evil scientist continued, "I estimate the need for five more capacitors

to saturate 85% of the population just for the North American target. But before full implementation, we must test the capacitor and examine the results of the first fielded and fully operational system in the American Southwest."

"How soon can you fire the capacitor?" Axxes asked.

"Very soon, Mr. Axxes," came the reply from the toxic scientist. "I estimate in less than 72 hours. I am flying out to the site this afternoon in the Copterjet."

The board of directors around the table looked at each other and nodded approvingly.

"And how long to start seeing results?" Axxes replied, his impatience rising to the surface. These plans had begun nearly a year ago.

Kaustik was prepared: "That is more difficult to calculate. The microscopic acid flakes we're releasing into the clean air should remain stable for up to five days depending on factors such as weather, temperature and such. I am estimating saturation into the human population in the targeted nine states of around 12.5% of the released cloud. Based on our studies, the average human throat and lungs will start showing signs of scorching within a week."

Dr. Kaustik was smiling proudly over his latest harmful experiment, and the positive results he anticipated, although none could see beneath his massive

white moustache nor behind his mouthpiece permanent-ly attached to his face that allowed him to breathe.

"This is indeed excellent news, Doctor," Axxes said with an evil grin. "Your notes indicate zero chance of detection... You assured me that diagnosis of the symptoms will place the blame on greenhouse gases and vehicle emissions. You understand, Doctor, that this is critical to the success of our plan — we cannot be traced as the sole source of the poisoned air."

"Of this, I can assure you," Kaustik hissed through his mouthpiece.

Nathan Axxes nodded in approval and turned to his board of executives.

"Gentlemen, based on this information, we are ready to launch Project Phoenix," Axxes said, now standing for all to see how serious he was about his latest plan. "I want finalized designs of the air purification sys-tems to counter our deadly cloud of invisible toxins by close of business this Friday. I expect all related accounting, resource and financial projections reworked until they are flawless."

"Um, sir," spoke a nervous young upstart in a dark black suit with a dark purple tie that wasn't quite straight. "I'm a little concerned over something... What if we can't engineer a cleansing machine for the toxic air?"

Axxes turned to the confused executive, leaned in menacingly and raised his lip in a sneer. With squinted eyes, the heartless, long-silver-haired tyrant spoke, "You simple-minded, ignorant dolt." Axxes sneered as his teeth ground together angrily. "You just don't get it, do you? I don't want you idiots designing these multi-billion-dollar systems to actually work! All we're going to do is shut off the Phoenix capacitors to make the fools on Capitol Hill think that our purifiers are actually cleansing the air. In reality, we're just building overly complex and overly expensive machines that literally do nothing at all while we rake in billions so the worthless people on this worthless planet can breathe clean air... That is, as long as they pay us to keep our systems running."

"Oh, um, yes, sir," the embarrassed and visually terrified junior director said apologetically. "So, what you're saying is the people in North America will have to pay to keep our purifier stations running — even though they're not really doing anything? That's genius!"

A huge smile slowly crept across Mr. Axxes' face when he saw that his cowering, sweat-covered associate finally understood the immenseness of the plan.

"North America is just the start, you idiot! I want this project running worldwide by the end of the year.

People have been paying for the clean water they've been drinking for years now and I've made millions from it," Axxes snarled. "But when they have to pay for air — when they have to pay for every single time they draw a breath — I will finally have them right where I want them!"

"We've been w-w-walking for days, Mesquite... I'm tired, let's rest," pleaded Sequoia, the portly brown bear cub, to his wolf pup friend.

"Yeah, and I'm thirsty!" piped in Juniper, the small five-month-old female black-footed ferret.

"Geez," Mesquite said as he turned to face his weary pals. "Alright, everyone, let's take a break over there in the shade of that scrub oak. I guess some of you just can't keep up," he added with a sour note while glaring back at Sequoia and Juniper.

The five animals tromped a few yards to the cooler shelter offered by a scraggly cluster of small trees.

"You guys need to toughen up," Mesquite said while hiding the fact that he was just as relieved as the rest of them to take a break and get out of the hot sun.

Mesquite always tried to make sure the others did not see any sign of weakness as he always thought of himself as their leader. "You don't see me or Cedar being a cry-baby," he added and nodded his nose toward the badger cub, looking for some support.

"Don't try to buddy-up with me," Cedar snarled back.

"This trek toward the south in the middle of the day was your stupid idea. I'm tired, I'm thirsty and I'm starting to get hungry."

Just then Aspen, the fledgling peregrine falcon, fluttered down from a tree limb and landed in the shade with the rest of the group. After she tucked her little wings up under her body she spoke: "Mesquite, just because you're always in front doesn't mean you know where you're going nor what you're doing!" Aspen liked to make sure Mesquite didn't always appear to be so self-confident.

"Since all of you are stuck down here on the ground, and I can fly around and get a much better view, I can tell you all that there is a really big canyon up ahead and a big river cuts through the bottom of it," Aspen continued while Mesquite gritted his teeth. "We need to head down this trail up ahead if we want to get a drink; otherwise it could be miles until we see any water."

The wolf pup spoke to cover up the fact that he was in fact a bit lost: "I know there's a river down there, Aspen, and I don't need a show-off bird flying around to tell me about it, either! I was about to take us all down there anyway!"

"No you weren't!" Cedar said defiantly, calling Mesquite on his bluff. "You were lost again!"

"Was not!" the wolf shot back, trying his best to defend himself.

Sequoia rolled his eyes back in disbelief. "Oh, j-j-just shut up all of you!" the bear interrupted with his usual stuttering speech impediment he'd had since birth.

"Can't we go one mile without some sort of b-b-bickering? I just want to sit here and feel the air blow through my fur and try to p-p-pick up on the scents around this place. I might just be able to sniff out a trash can full of f-f-food or maybe even a campsite!"

The thought of food brought the group to a pause and a mutual focus on something to take away the nagging in their empty stomachs and a welcome distraction from all the quibbling. Sequoia's nose was quite good at smelling food sources from a long distance and the little group of orphaned animals often relied upon him to find their meals.

It stayed quiet for a few minutes as the group sat there in the shade cooling off and resting their weary feet. They had been on the move for several days — heading south following signs revealed to them by nature itself or perhaps by the shaman chief who had given them their powers.

Back in Colorado, they had come upon a pile of pinecones that had fallen and somehow formed the perfect shape of an arrow pointing southwest. They

followed that clue and stayed on that course for over two hundred miles and into Utah until they came across another unmistakable directional shape — this one formed randomly by rocks that had fallen from the cliffs above onto the trail they were on and made another unmistakable arrow, this time pointing south. Unknowingly, they had crossed the border into Arizona just two days ago.

Cedar broke the silence. "I was just thinking that this little quest we're on is ridiculous. I mean, we've been on the move for weeks and haven't done anything besides roam these wastelands."

"What are you saying? Do you want to quit?" Juniper inquired, a little scared at the answer she might get from the disgruntled badger.

"Well, yeah," Cedar replied. "We never asked to take on this responsibility. We're way too young to handle this. Why us? Why me? Sometimes, I just want to take this amulet off and go make a life for myself somewhere and be left alone."

"It's too late now," Juniper said. "You can't just give up on the world! We can't turn a blind eye and watch the earth slowly die."

"Look, Cedar," Aspen added, "all we have now is each other. I don't like it any more than the rest of you. I should be hanging out with other fliers and not watching

over you grounders. I know I was born for greatness — and I guess you all were, too."

Aspen grasped the enchanted necklace hanging under her chin. "This gift we were given is a great one. We can make a difference and balance the scales around here. I can't do this by myself," the pint-sized peregrine falcon said.

"Do you smell anything yet, Sequoia?" Mesquite asked rather loudly, hoping to change the subject.

"Not food. But I can smell g-g-gas from humans," the little bear replied.

"Eeeew! Yuck! You're smelling people farts!" Cedar declared, and the whole gang burst out laughing.

"N-n-not that, you idiots!" Sequoia shot back. "You know, like they u-u-use for f-f-fuel."

Cedar calmed himself enough to ask another question. "Maybe it's a campfire or a restaurant!"

"There aren't any restaurants way out here, Cedar, you stupid hole digger!" Aspen declared.

"What did you just say to me?" Cedar snarled back and started over towards the little bird, making it clear that she could see his teeth.

Aspen flittered up to a branch out of reach of her angry young friend. "You heard me, badger-boy. My momma always told me that those with feathers are also those with brains!"

Juniper jumped up from where she was sitting and spoke, "Would you all be quiet, please! Go on, Sequoia... What's this fuel you're smelling?"

"Shh! Listen!" Sequoia bellowed.

The animals turned their heads and tilted their ears to try to hear what their friend heard.

"I hear it! And I smell it now, too!" Mesquite proclaimed. "It's like a high pressure burst of gas or something!"

Just then, a large rainbow-colored hot-air balloon with a big basket tied below it rose in front of them over the horizon. It was huge. Startled at first, the animal orphans all jumped back in the cover of the bushes to hide from the two humans piloting the giant, slow-moving aircraft.

The man in the basket reached up and pulled a lever that released a shot of propane, which immediately burst into flames over their heads and filled the balloon with hot air, giving the humans another slow rise in elevation. The woman on board raised a camera to her eye and starting taking snapshots of the landscape below.

"Do you think they saw us?" Juniper asked worriedly.

"Do you think they've got food on board?" Sequoia inquired.

Mesquite took charge again. "No, they didn't see us and even if they did have food up there, what're you

going to do? Go out there and give them your sad puppy-dog eyes and hope that they'll throw you a sandwich?"

"That's not a bad idea!" Sequoia said and started to step out from under the scrub oak bushes before Mesquite grabbed him by the tail with his mouth and hauled him back.

"Knock it off, all of you!" Cedar snapped. "Stay quiet and stay hidden. They'll be gone soon."

The balloon floated silently over the animal squad and, carried by the wind, slowly drifted off in the opposite direction from which it came. An occasional burst of propane catching fire above the humans' heads broke the otherwise complete silence of the contraption.

After a couple of minutes the gang crept out from the safety of their shelter.

"That was a close one!" Mesquite said. "Your sniffer saved us again, Sequoia!"

At that moment, they heard a scream come from the direction of the hot-air balloon. The animals scurried to a clearing to get a better view.

A fast-moving, high-tech aircraft that looked like half helicopter and half fighter-jet rocketed past the balloon, just missing it by a few feet.

The whirlwind of air in the wake of the high-speed flying machine caused the balloon's structure to buckle.

The humans were thrown into the bottom of the giant wicker gondola hanging below. One of the sides of the balloon caved in far enough that the heat from the burner caught the silky material on fire.

The man and the woman on board were desperately holding onto each other as well as the swirling, spinning basket while they screamed for help. Their balloon careened out of control and plummeted toward a very deep ravine, leaving a smoky trail behind them in the sky.

"Move out!" Mesquite shouted as he leapt off the large flat rock he was standing on.

The animals immediately responded and while running toward the falling balloon, each transformed into their super-selves as bolts of turquoise-colored lightning streaked out from their amulets.

Mesquite, now transformed and clearly the leader of the group, assertively barked out orders with clarity and confidence.

"Aspen! See what you can do to slow the descent of that balloon!"

The woman-sized peregrine falcon shot off with incredible speed toward the helpless humans, a wake of dust and feathers streaming behind her.

"Juniper! Go after that aircraft! You're the only one fast enough to keep up with it. But do not engage! Report back to us when you see where it sets down!"

The black-footed ferret took off like a missile cruising six inches off the ground. Juniper had to use all four feet to attain such a high velocity, nearly breaking the sound barrier. A long, bright bluish-green streak

followed behind her as she zoomed after the Copterjet that was now nearly out of sight over a rocky ridge a few miles away.

"Sequoia! Cedar! Let's give Aspen some back-up!" With that last command from the alpha-wolf, the powered-up animals launched into action, hurdling over rocks and shrubs in a desperate attempt to save the people crashing toward earth.

Meanwhile, Aspen had caught up with the hot-air balloon on its death spiral into the canyon. Folding her wings back tightly against her body, she went into a high-speed dive and swooped down on it. She flung her large talons forward at the last instant and grabbed onto the collapsed canopy.

The nylon ripped and tore, but she had enough of it clenched in her feet to get a good, firm grasp. The balloon came to a sudden stop and then, flapping her powerful wings, she strained to pull the destroyed balloon and its terrified occupants toward the safety of the cliffside.

The balloon was surprisingly heavy, and Aspen had exerted too much energy just getting to the balloon. It was all she could do bring it up a few dozen feet and to the side of the canyon. She was losing her grip and she knew she couldn't make it all the way to the safety of the ground next to the canyon.

Glancing to her side, she spotted a rocky outcropping not too far away that looked strong enough to hold the balloon. With her beak tightly clenched, Aspen pushed herself hard for one last-ditch effort to save the people dangling in the basket below her. Her wings hammered away at the air and she managed to lift them up and over, a little more, a little higher, until she finally reached the overhanging cliff face.

She managed to position the shredded balloon canopy around the rock cluster enough for it to become entangled and keep it from falling — as long as the ropes holding the basket held tight.

Aspen nearly collapsed once she was able to let go of the balloon; she had over-exerted herself, and she struggled to stay on the rock-tower herself. She could hear the humans hanging below screaming for help but there was nothing more she could do.

Mesquite, Cedar and Sequoia finally arrived at the scene. From their position on the cliff face 25 feet above, they could see that Aspen had rescued the balloonists from certain death, but now they were dangling dangerously from an outcropping of rocks that jutted up and out from the massive ravine. The humans would need further help getting safely to firm ground.

Mesquite turned to Sequoia and Cedar, anxious to

rescue the stranded humans and their peregrine friend. "Here's the plan! Cedar, go back a few paces and dig a tunnel 25 feet down and then over to the cliff's edge. If you judge it right, you should come out level with the basket those humans are stuck in. But be careful — don't tunnel too fast toward the edge or you'll end up falling in the canyon yourself."

Cedar stepped back from the edge and summoned his powers into his enormous claws. Immediately, they started glowing a bright turquoise color. Then the man-badger plunged them into the ground, tearing through the rock and carving a tunnel big enough for a bobsled. Stone and dirt flew back from the hole like snow out of a snow blower.

"What about me, Mesquite?" Sequoia bellowed, his stuttering now completely gone. "What can I do? I gotta help those guys!"

Mesquite looked up at the mighty bear looming ten feet tall over him. "Once Cedar bores that tunnel, we need a bridge of some kind to that outcropping..."

Before Mesquite could finish his sentence, the giant grizzly bolted off to find something that would work as a platform out to the humans.

Mesquite motioned to the very edge of the cliff and bent down on one knee, calling out to Aspen clutching the top of the rock column.

"Aspen!" he shouted. "We're on our way, just hang in there!"

She glanced up at him and nodded.

Just then, the sheer cliff wall next to the stranded humans and their unseen bird-woman savior above them exploded in a shower of rocks and sand. Cedar had dug down and over almost perfectly in line with the hanging basket. The large hole he tunneled just a few feet away from them was the entrance to a safe passageway leading up and away to solid ground.

The people cowering on the floor of the large wicker box tied to the ruined remains of their hot-air balloon were still too scared to move. Every shift of their bodies caused the basket to swing and creak, and the ropes, stretched and taut, were barely holding it to the rocks above. They were ready to snap any second.

With his large, powerful arms, Cedar hoisted himself back out of the tunnel at the spot where he had first started his incredible dig. As he wiped off the dirt from his fur, he turned to Mesquite. "Where's that bear with that bridge?"

That's when they heard a tremendous cracking sound as if a thunderclap had just exploded a few feet away. It startled Mesquite enough so that he went into a defensive stance and raised his spear as a safeguard to protect himself.

Cedar, also crouched as if ready to fight, asked aloud, "What was that? It sounded like an explosion!"

Through a cloud of dust undoubtedly raised by whatever had caused the concussion, Sequoia emerged holding something nearly as massive as he was. When he approached his wolf and badger partners, relaxing from their aggressive poses, it became clear that he was holding a huge and heavy slice of rock.

"Sorry about the noise, fellas," the mighty grizzly spoke. "The trees around here are too small — I had to rip this wedge of limestone off the mountain over there." Then, proudly holding the 1500-pound rock like a giant misshapen surfboard next to him so the others could get a better look, Sequoia asked, "Well, do you think it'll work?"

Mesquite and Cedar looked at the huge sliver of limestone, then at each other, and simultaneously replied, "Too big!"

Mesquite, knowing time was of the essence, spoke quickly, "Sequoia, hold that thing still while Cedar and I carve away the excess stone!"

Cedar activated his glowing claws again and started chiseling away at the edges to reduce the rock's girth. Mesquite joined Cedar by using his spear, the tip glowing brightly, cutting and slashing away with quick, decisive jabs and thrusts. In seconds, the massive

stone sliver was cut down to a more manageable size.

Sequoia shoved the smaller piece, still ten feet long, down into the hole. Cedar and Mesquite jumped down in the tunnel behind it and, with great effort, managed to slide the heavy piece toward the tunnel opening that plummeted to the canyon's bottom a half-mile below.

"Okay," Mesquite said, catching his breath. "I estimate it's seven feet over to the rock column the humans are stuck on. This slice of stone is about ten feet long — that gives us three feet to spare so we need to leave no less than a foot on this side, and the rest has to set on that ledge on the rock column so they can walk over."

"Are you sure that little ledge can hold this thing?" Cedar asked.

"It's going to have to," came the reply.

From the end of the tunnel, they could see the balloon basket just a few feet in front of them. They could hear the people inside, terrified but alive. But between the humans and the tunnel's edge was a drop-off even the Natural Forces team couldn't survive if they fell.

"We have one shot at this," Cedar said to his wolf companion. "If we shove this thing too hard and it goes too far, it could either glance off the rock column and fall to the canyon floor or, worse, it could hit the basket they're hanging in…"

"And if we don't shove it hard enough, the weight of it will be too much for us to hold and it's going to drop..." Mesquite added.

Aspen, a few feet above them, propped herself up, assessed the situation, and called over to them, "You better hurry, guys, these ropes won't hold much longer!"

"We've got to get his right, buddy," Mesquite said to Cedar, who was positioning himself for a big push of the rock slice. "Let's do this on three. One...two...three!"

With that, the wolf and the badger heaved the segment of limestone with all their might. It shot out of the tunnel opening in a cloud of dust and sand, landing with a loud thud perfectly on the ledge of the stone column across the chasm. Their stone bridge was in place and solidly attached.

The boys gave themselves high-fives and retreated back out of the tunnel.

Aspen stood up and then leapt off the stone column perch, spread her wings, and had just enough energy to fly up to the cliff top where her friends waited. The boys were glad to see she was doing better and they hugged her as soon as she landed.

Shortly after, they moved as one to the rim of the canyon and peered down to see if the humans had gotten up the nerve to come out of their tethered wicker cradle and move across the improvised bridge and into

the tunnel that Cedar had dug.

To their surprise, that's exactly what was happening 25 feet below them. The man was helping the woman and they both skittishly managed to get across the rock bridge on their hands and knees.

Knowing the humans were safe, the foursome quickly set off so as not to be seen by the people they had just rescued. They wanted to keep their identities a secret.

Within seconds, they were out of sight and on a quest to find Juniper and the heartless pilot of the aircraft that had nearly killed two people.

Meanwhile, four miles away, Juniper watched undetected as the Copterjet flown by Dr. Kaustik slowed to a hover and in a smooth, sweeping arc descended into a gorge.

The steep, rocky sides surrounding it made for an ideal place for secretive activities but was also a very difficult place to reach. Kaustik, a skilled pilot with remarkable confidence, slid the rather large aircraft in between the cliff walls and with the push of a button from the cockpit, two giant false doors to the cavern quickly opened.

The Copterjet fluttered with hardly a sound into the concealed cave entrance. Two hatches in the bottom of the advanced plane swung open and the landing gear deployed just seconds before Kaustik set down the airframe inside the secret cave. The giant, disguised doors to the large cave quickly closed behind, ensuring nobody would find them.

The whirring engines came to a gradual stop just as the door in the back of the Copterjet lowered to the ground like a large ramp. Four Soldierjacks exited first,

three of them carrying equipment and supplies while the fourth unloaded a large wire cage filled with rabbits. The vile doctor descended the ramp last, followed by his ever-present SPIDER that he was always connected to with breathing hoses.

"SJ-One, status report!" Kaustik shouted as soon as he set foot on the steel-hardened cave floor.

A larger Soldierjack with a black band on its left arm and a more advanced helmet, clearly a commander unit, stepped forward to greet the newly arrived visitor.

In a computer-generated voice, SJ-One gave his report: "Zzt! On schedule, Doctor. Initiation estimations on track. Cavern wall structural integrity at 99%. Product generation at 65%. Disparity in predicted biometric..."

Kaustik raised one of his gloved hands and cut off his underling in mid-sentence. "Enough. Well done. Now get back to work. I want to inspect the microbes in the lab." With his SPIDER in tow, the white-robed doctor turned and headed off down a tunnel recently carved into the cave.

The cavern itself was immense. The chamber, naturally dug but artificially expanded into the surrounding mountainside, simply dwarfed the rather large Copter-jet parked in the middle of it. A flurry of activity was going on.

All around, Soldierjacks were busy working. Some were driving forklifts or small carts towing trailers filled with equipment or gravel. Several were laboring on the cave itself — reinforcing the cave walls with large beams or setting steel flooring. Still others were setting up computer stations and running diagnostics.

A wall of generators along the far wall kept power pumping into the solitary area and served as a recharging station for those Soldierjacks who had drained their internal power source.

In another area, the robotic workforce was busy in the final stages of assembling the massive grinder that crushed the rock and gravel into a fine powder.

Most of the Soldierjacks were toward the back of the cavern, putting the finishing touches on the huge, intricate capacitor itself — the very machine that would launch the toxic dust out through a long, skinny tube and up into the atmosphere where it would mix with the air and burn the lungs of all who would breathe it.

In the lab, Dr. Kaustik was using an electron microscope to examine samples of the deadly dust. His SPIDER was at his side, cleansing the lungs of its host as always. The doctor would often turn to it and type notes into the keyboard on its face.

Suddenly, a large crashing sound echoed through the cave. Kaustik and the SPIDER bolted from the lab

to see what had happened.

Along the north wall of the cave, a Soldierjack had dropped a 20-foot steel girder from the forklift it was operating while hoisting it into place. The heavy I-beam had crashed to the steel floor and cut several power cables that snaked across the floor.

Kaustik was furious. "You idiot!" he screamed at the emotionless robot. "That little accident just cost us another couple hours!"

Enraged, he turned to face the SPIDER behind him and quickly disconnected his breathing hoses. The tap of a key dislodged a small oxygen tank from beneath the SPIDER that Dr. Kaustik immediately hooked his breathing tubes into and then slung the strap attached to the tank over his shoulder. He could breathe this way for up to three hours. With two more quick keystrokes, he set the SPIDER into attack mode.

It instantly rose up and extended its legs with a series of clicking sounds. Hidden compartments opened and protective shield plating snapped into place around the air purification tubes on its back as well as over the computer components. From below the head of the mechanical arthropod, a twin-barreled cannon lowered and locked into place.

Kaustik pointed toward the clumsy Soldierjack and yelled for the SPIDER to strike.

The six-legged mechanical monster scuttled across the cavern with stunning speed. Soldierjacks fled out of its path toward the unsuspecting worker repositioning his forklift into place to lift the steel beam it had accidentally dropped.

The SPIDER leaped and landed next to the forklift. It raised its front right leg and in one lethal, powerful stroke jammed the huge, sharp tip into the Soldierjack's torso. As the android twitched about, the SPIDER flung it out from the forklift and across the cave floor.

Sparks erupted from the torn body of the Soldierjack as it attempted to stand and defend itself. But the SPIDER was too quick. In seconds it was on him again and flung the hapless laborer against the nearest cave wall. The Soldierjack crashed to the floor but was somehow still moving.

The SPIDER clamored over to it, reared up and fired a toxic stream of venom from both nozzles of its gun directly at the Soldierjack's chest. The lethal liquid quickly ate away at the robot, dissolving the upper half of the Soldierjack into a bubbling, gaseous puddle.

"Return!" Dr. Kaustik shouted to his SPIDER from across the cave. The horrifying mechanical enforcer turned to its master and strode over, its heavy pointed legs clack-clack-clacking against the metal floor.

When it stopped in front of Kaustik, the doctor set it back in normal mode and plugged his breathing tubes back into it.

"Excellent, my pet," the doctor said as he stroked the menacing metal monster as if it were alive.

Then he turned toward the Soldierjacks mindlessly returning to their duties, "Let that be a lesson to all of you! Now clean up that worthless pile of scrap metal, fix the damage it caused and get us back on schedule!"

With that, the doctor and his attached mechanical partner turned and headed down the hallway to finish his work in the lab.

CHAPTER 5

Transformed back into their younger forms, Mesquite, Cedar, Sequoia and Aspen scampered along the canyon's ridgeline in the direction where they had last seen Juniper.

"I hope we can f-f-find her," Sequoia called out to the others. "She could be f-f-far away."

"Don't worry, fur-butt," Aspen replied. "We'll find her or she'll find us."

Bounding up and over the craggy terrain, the four-some was growing weary. They made sure to scan in all directions along the way; even a super-powered ferret wasn't very large and if she was going full speed she could very well be in the next county by now. After nearly three miles, they stopped in the shadow of an over-hanging rock.

"Let's rest here a bit," Mesquite said. "Aspen, maybe you can fly up and get a better view from the sky. Maybe you can see her."

"Sure. Let me catch my breath first," she replied.

Cedar spoke up with a parched voice, "Guys, we really need to get some water soon. I don't think any of us

are going to get very far without a drink of water."

"He's right," Sequoia added. "I'm p-p-parched."

Mesquite, embarrassed that he hadn't thought of the condition of the others, spoke up. "Okay, how about we go just a little further and then we can start heading down into the canyon to the river at the bottom for a good, long drink?"

The others nodded their heads in agreement, but they all knew that if Juniper was still somewhere up on the flat surface area and they were all heading down into the canyon, the odds of finding each other were very slim.

That's when they heard a faint sound off in the distance. Almost a whisper, they could make out someone crying out: "Guys! Hello! Where are you?"

"Juniper!" Sequoia shouted with his ears locked on the voice. He jumped up onto all four feet and headed off in her direction with the rest following closely behind.

Soon they were all calling out to her. "Juniper! Juniper!"

"Down here!" Juniper called out from halfway down in the canyon. "I'm down here!"

The foursome peered over the edge into the canyon below and spotted their little black-footed ferret friend, morphed back into a kit, several hundred feet below them.

"We'll come down to you!" Mesquite shouted. "Stay there!"

Aspen hopped over the ledge and fluttered down to her female friend in a matter of seconds. She wasn't a very good flyer in her younger form, but even she could handle a simple drop like that one. The boys meanwhile scampered about back and forth on the canyon's rim, looking for a trail of sorts that they could follow down into the canyon.

Cedar finally found a passage that would work and called out to his pals. "Guys! I found a way down!"

Mesquite and Sequoia trotted over to where the badger had already started downward and joined Cedar on his descent to the bottom. It took them about 30 minutes of carefully going over and around rocks, big and small, and avoiding the seemingly endless cactus and other pokey plants along the way. Finally they got to Juniper and Aspen who were waiting for them in the shade of a twisted pine tree.

"I know where the aircraft went," Juniper told the boys. "It's not far from here. We can be there in about an hour."

"Make that two hours," Cedar said. "We're gonna get some water first!"

Reunited, the five friends worked their way to the canyon's bottom and found relief in the cool but murky

water of the Colorado River that cut through it.

Being small, they had to find an area where the river's edge branched off into calmer pools so they could drink without being washed away. After a few minutes, they all had their fill and were feeling much better.

Mesquite, ready for action, turned to Juniper. "Okay, girl, where'd that dirtbag in that flying machine go?"

Juniper, happy to be the one with critical information who had successfully tracked the Copterjet, blurted out, "This way!"

The group followed after the little ferret and about a mile later they stopped when they came to a newly worn path along the canyon's bottom.

Mesquite lowered his snout to the ground, examining the footprints up close. Sequoia sniffed at the air, hoping to detect a tell-tale scent.

Then, at the same time, they spoke and said the very same thing, "I don't think these are human."

"I'm pretty sure we're on the backside of where the aircraft went into the secret cave," Juniper said. "Maybe this trail leads to a back door or something."

"It's worth a try!" Mesquite blurted. "C'mon everybody! Let's see where it goes."

Mesquite jumped out onto the trail and started following it before his friends could even reply.

"I have a bad feeling about this," Cedar grumbled to the others.

The five little critters were soon all together again, the animals walking shoulder to shoulder down the path, while Aspen fluttered along with them.

One side of the well-worn trail dropped off a few dozen feet to the rushing Colorado River below, the other tucked up against the red-stone cliff walls. After nearly a mile, it led directly into the back and very bottom of the cliff.

As they came around a rather tight bend and between two oddly placed boulders, they noticed a dark entrance to a cave that was loosely disguised by some shrubs. This caused the team to stop in their tracks and pause as they analyzed the situation.

Mesquite spoke first, "I say we go in. This has to be the secret entrance to their lair."

Cedar wasn't so sure. "Just like that?" he said. "Go barging right in? What if there's a trap? What if there are cameras?"

"You know, for a badger, you sure aren't very brave, are you?" Mesquite retorted.

"Oh, yeah, and for a wolf you're not real smart," Cedar fired back.

"Guys..." Aspen interrupted, but wasn't really heard.

The two arguing boys glared at each other.

"Uh, guys," Aspen said again, only louder. "Guys!" she finally screamed at the top of her lungs.

The four others turned their heads up to their falcon friend bobbing on a small branch of a small tree that hung over the trail. She had been flying from tree to tree above the group and suddenly noticed something rather peculiar in the loose sand of the track they were standing on.

"Maybe you grounders are too blind to see, but there's something rather weird about this trail we're on," Aspen said snobbishly.

"What are you t-t-talking about?" Sequoia stuttered.

"Well, I get a better view of the world from up here, of course..." she started.

"Yeah, yeah," Mesquite broke in. "Just say it, Aspen. You don't need to rub it in that you can fly every time you talk to us."

"Well, for quite some time now, I've been noticing large swirls in the sand," the little bird said, annoyed at the wolf pup's comment to her. "At first I thought maybe the rains had caused them, but I really think these are made by a living creature."

At this, all four animals turned to look down at the path beneath them. Juniper jumped up on Sequoia's back to get a better look.

"I see what she's sayin'!" Juniper said. "It's like the trail a snake leaves in the sand as they slither from side to side, only it's way too big to be a snake."

Mesquite looked up and down the trail, even raising his paw to look at the swirl mark underneath him. He could see what the girls were talking about — a swirling, pushing effect of the sand was visible in large, long, curving drifts that went from one side of the trail all the way over to the other. "What? That's crazy. There must be an explanation for this."

Just then the group was startled by the sound of a loud rattling noise: a very loud, very fast, rattling noise.

"What the..." was all Cedar could get out before a massive snake slithered out from behind one of the boulders in front of them. It was an impossibly large snake, unnatural for sure, and as its giant body crept out of the shadows and coiled around itself, the team could see clearly that it was an aggravated, super-sized rattlesnake.

Its head, with deeply set yellow eyes, was the size of a man's bicycle seat and its body, as round as a basketball, stretched the length of a school bus. The over-sized rattle on its tail resembled a bone-colored corn-cob and was shaking wildly back and forth.

The animals all slowly stepped backwards at the sight of the monstrous serpent. Then it spoke: "What

issss it you want, little morsels?" the mighty rattler said with a deep, creepy hiss.

"N-n-nothing," Mesquite stammered - very much like Sequoia's speech impediment. The intimidated wolf pup continued, his words trembling from his lips, "We're just passing through."

The little wolf's obvious lie angered the snake. "You lie!" the snake roared, raising his body higher and swaying back and forth. "I don't like liarssss...except for how they tasssste!"

Sequoia, feeling brave and being the largest of the team, stepped forward on nervous legs. He doubted he could morph into his powerful self before the snake struck. But he figured the snake had valuable information nonetheless.

"You're the b-b-biggest snake we've ever seen!" the little bear said, clearly feeding into the reptile's ego. "How d-d-did you get so big?"

The snake flicked his tongue at the bear as if to sample Sequoia's flavor. It smiled and answered, "Oh, I'm a sssspecial sssspecies, little bear. I'm a product of the doctor's crossss-breeding."

"What doctor? What c-c-cross-breeding?" Sequoia asked. He was confused, but glad they were at least communicating.

The enormous snake paused for a second, but then

realized any secrets he may reveal to five tiny forest creatures surely couldn't be harmful. They had to get past him, anyway.

"Doctor Kausssstik, of courssssse," the snake hissed. "My mother wassss a diamondback and my father wasssss a python. I was born in hisssss lab, right here.

The animals looked at each other, perplexed.

Sequoia probed further, hoping to avoid a confrontation. "Who is th-th-this Dr. Kaustik, sir? Can we meet him? Can we see-see-see his lab?"

"Never!" the snake screamed and shook his tail even faster, the rattling noise echoing off the cliff walls. "I don't let anyone passsss. He keeps me here sssssso nobody may passsss!"

"Well, we really need to get past, sir," Mesquite said. "We need to get in that cave. We're on a mission!"

"Mesquite!" Cedar scolded in a harsh whisper. "What are you doing? You're going to get us all killed!"

The snake was growing more and more angry.

"I'd like to ssssee you try to get passsst me!" the serpent said. "I am the fassssstest there is. Nobody gets passsst me!"

"Oh, I don't think you're that fast, sir!" Mesquite replied. "I know someone that's faster than you. How about we make a deal?"

"No one is fasssster than me!" the half-breed snake

bragged. "I am a product of sssscience and I am the fassstest there is!"

"Wanna bet?" the little wolf proposed.

"Sssure thing, morsel!" the snake confidently replied. "I have taken down every ssssingle animal in these parts. I am the king of sssnakes!"

Mesquite decided to push his adversary further. His plan was coming together nicely.

"I bet even our youngest and smallest animal is faster than you!" Mesquite said, turning to look at Juniper who clearly did not want to be volunteered at all. Mesquite winked at her as if not to worry. She snarled back at him.

"Bah!" the snake shot back. It turned its huge triangular-shaped head and stared at Juniper. "That little ferret? I will sssswallow her whole!"

"Here's the deal," the pup proposed. "If she can get past you, then you have to admit that you're not the fastest and let all of us pass."

The snake squinted its eyes even tighter as he looked at Mesquite and thought about the wolfling's offer. Thinking that this little game might be fun and that chasing his meal would make for a nice change from the hand-delivered pile of rabbits Dr. Kaustik usually fed him every week, the snake agreed.

"It'sssss a deal, you sssstupid clump of fur," the

giant snake said offensively. A huge smile slowly spread across its scaly face, revealing two fangs the size of fat pencils. "And when I'm done with her, I'm coming for you, boy!"

Mesquite spoke as he walked backward to his team, "Fine. Whatever. Okay, let's start this on the count of three!"

Juniper inched her way forward and glared at the little wolf, "Thanks a lot!" she spat. "This better work!"

Mesquite started the countdown, "One!"

The mighty snake loosened its coils a bit to give it room to stretch and tensed its muscles for a massive strike.

"Two!" the wolf barked out as Sequoia, Cedar and Aspen huddled together towards the back of the trail, hoping their littlest friend could beat the genetically altered half-rattler, half-python.

Mesquite looked at Juniper and nodded his head as an indication for her to morph into her super form. "Three!"

Brilliant flashes of turquoise light erupted from Juniper's amulet as she instantly transformed inside a sparkling, swirling cloud from her youthful self into the super-powered humanoid ferret three times her previous size.

The snake, temporarily blinded by the magical light

show bursting around Juniper, swooped in...too late.

Juniper leaped into the air, right over the snake's first lunge. Spinning acrobatically in the air, she landed safely several feet away.

The snake swung around for another strike. "Ssssome ssssort of trickery! No matter! You can't essssscape me, girl!" the snake shrieked.

Like a lightning strike, the colossal serpent struck again. Juniper managed to dodge the beast for the second time, rolling and spinning under its attack.

"C'mon, big-boy," Juniper jeered. "I thought science could beat nature! Let's see what you got!"

Riled, the snake coiled all of its length into a tight spring. Hissing and baring its ten-inch-long fangs, the reptile did a fake lunge. Juniper responded by moving to her left, but realizing it was a feint, she steadied herself for the actual strike. By then, the snake had already thrust. It shot forward like a bullet train.

Juniper flipped up, put her hands on the snake's snout, and using its own momentum twirled back and over the snake like a gymnast. The mighty serpent struck the ground with a thud and cloud of dust.

The fleeting ferret jumped up on the snake's back, ran down the course of it and then leaped up on top of the boulder the serpent had slithered out from behind.

By now, the snake was furious. Juniper's friends,

safely out of range, were cheering her on, which angered the mighty rattler even more.

"I had thought I might break a sweat, Mr. Snake," Juniper teased. "You sure you're fast?"

Sneering, the snake readied for one final blow. "You'll ssssee, little morsel, you'll ssssee!"

Diving hard, the huge serpent sprang at its quarry with all of its might.

Juniper dove for the ground and the snake adjusted its course, tracking her perfectly. Spring-boarding off the sand, the super-powered ferret shot back the opposite way, twisting and contorting her body almost like a snake herself.

Then, as if in slow motion, Juniper darted right through the open mouth of the snake during its lunge and safely out the other side. The giant beast slammed its mouth shut, catching nothing but air.

Distracted from its course, blinded by anger, and unable to stop, the snake smashed headlong with full fury into the boulder Juniper had just been standing on.

A horrendous cracking sound echoed out into the canyon. The snake, completely dazed, made a last swaying, uncontrolled, circular motion and then fell unconscious to the sand with a solid thud.

Loud cheers erupted from Juniper's four friends as they rushed in to hug their champion who, sensing the

danger was gone, had already transformed back into her smaller version.

"Way to go, Juniper! I knew you could do it!" Mesquite acclaimed.

Juniper reached up and grabbed the small wolf by the ear. "Don't you ever do that to me again!"

The entrance to the cave wasn't very large - about the size of a man. The five animals approached it very cautiously.

Peering slowly around one of the boulders, they could see that hidden in the shadows at the top corner of the opening was a video camera. Its lens was aimed directly at the trail entrance and someone was certainly on the other end watching everything.

Behind it, about ten feet inside the cave entryway, a steel door barred the way.

"We need to get in there, guys," Mesquite said. "Huddle up, I have a plan."

The four others exhaled heavily and rolled their eyes upward — most plans thought up by their wolf-pup friend seemed to get them in trouble. They gathered around him in a semi-circle. Mesquite went on and on about his elaborate scheme and even used his paw to draw details in the sand.

Aspen, looking down on the group from a perched position on an overhanging branch above, realized this was one of Mesquite's craziest ideas yet.

"Forget this," she thought to herself and flew down to the ground opposite Mesquite, who was still yammering on about his elaborate plan to get in the cave undetected. Once there, she started collecting leaves and twigs in her mouth and feet.

Cedar, Sequoia and Juniper all stopped paying attention to Mesquite and glanced behind him to watch Aspen instead.

With her beak full, Aspen flew as best she could straight up to the camera in the cave. She started to interweave the sticks and dead leaves right in front of the camera. Once she was done, she flew back down, gathered some more and repeated the process.

On her third trip to the ground, Cedar spoke up, interrupting Mesquite who had no idea Aspen hadn't been paying attention to him for the past three minutes. "Aspen! What do you think you're doing? They can see everything you're doing!"

By now, all four animals were peeking around the boulder to see what their little bird buddy was doing.

Aspen glared back at them and revealed her actions in a harsh whisper, "Isn't it obvious? Whoever is watching this camera thinks some stupid bird is just building a nest that just so happens to be blocking their view. They will send somebody out here to scare me off and take down the nest. When they do that, we all

sneak inside while the door's open."

The others looked at each other in amazement. Simultaneously, they all spoke. "That'll work!"

"Or you guys can try another of Mesquite's lamebrained ideas," Aspen replied back, much to Mesquite's dismay.

"N-n-no," Sequoia said, "we're good. Let's go with your plan!"

Aspen flew back up with another load for her fake nest. It was now almost completely obscuring the camera's view.

Aspen turned to the others, "Okay, guys! Get in here; they can't see us! Hide on each side of the door!"

The foursome bolted into the cave, split up, and hid in the shadows next to the steel door. Aspen flew down and joined the others. They didn't have to wait long.

From inside the cave they could hear heavy footsteps approaching. Two weighty bipeds were coming. Their steps stopped at the other side of the door. Then a small "beep" was heard and suddenly the steel door slid open.

Two Soldierjacks carrying Flamesaws — half chainsaw and half flamethrower devices that they used for clearing forests — stepped out into the cave opening. One of them headed out into the sunlight outside the chamber, scanning the area for anything out of place.

Fortunately, the giant snake lay unconscious behind one of the big boulders and out of immediate view.

The other Soldierjack walked up to the camera covered with Aspen's false nest. Reaching up with his weapon, he managed to knock the nest down without much effort.

Meanwhile, the Natural Forces team, well hidden and too small to be seen, ducked inside once the door had opened and the two robots came out.

"Zzt! All clear," one Soldierjack said to the other. They turned around and headed back inside.

The youngsters scampered down the newly carved tunnel, hugging the walls as they moved in hopes of not being spotted. They turned a corner and disappeared inside what appeared to be a storage room.

The back of the room was the original rocky cave wall itself; the other three walls were assembled by man, or machine, with steel supports and thin aluminum walls. Inside, stacked boxes, papers, various sorts of equipment and extra computers filled most of it. A hutch of rabbits was placed in the corner.

"Okay, wh-wh-what is this place?" Sequoia said to the others. "I don't like th-th-this one bit."

"Me neither!" Cedar agreed.

Juniper piped in, "Why would someone build a secret cave way out here with all this security? These guys

are up to no good for sure."

"Did you guys notice anything unusual about those two guards?" Mesquite asked. Getting no immediate reply, he continued, "They weren't human. They were robots!"

Aspen, who had flown up and landed on a tall cardboard box, reinforced Mesquite's observation. "That explains a bit more about that giant jerk of a reptile that almost ate Juniper. Snakes use their tongues to detect heat from animals. Those robots don't really give off any heat at all, so that gigantic snake out there who's going to wake up with a gigantic headache is the perfect protector of the backdoor. Anything robotic he lets go by and anything animal – or human – he either devours or scares away."

Mesquite wanted to put everything together in his head. "Okay, so we know the aircraft that almost killed those people landed on the other side of this cave, right? And we know they want this place kept secret. They have high-tech equipment, heavily armed robot guards and we all can smell trouble brewing. Now, let's find out exactly what they're up to!"

"I think we should split up," Mesquite said.

Juniper turned to Cedar and groaned, "I knew he was going to say that."

The wolf-child continued, "Us boys will take the corridor to the left, you girls go to the right. Let's see what we can find out and then meet back here in ten minutes."

"Whoa, whoa, whoa," Aspen declared. "Why is it always the boys and the girls?"

"What?!" Mesquite replied angrily.

"Why do the teams always have to consist of you boys versus us girls?" Aspen said.

"Oh, for cryin' out loud, Aspen..." Mesquite replied.

"Yeah, why are the teams always the same?" Juniper jumped in, noticing it was getting on Mesquite's nerves.

"We want Cedar on our team," Aspen added. "You and Sequoia can be a team, and we'll be a team. What do you think, Cedar? Want to be on our team?"

Cedar looked at the girls and then back at the boys. "You know, I don't really want to be on any team," he said gruffly.

Sequoia, hurt a little by not being chosen over his badger companion, cut in, "Hey, what am I, ch-ch-chopped liver?"

"I can't believe we're even having this conversation!" Mesquite snapped. "Okay, fine. You three go together and we big boys will be a team on our own. Meet back here in ten minutes."

The group split into two groups and headed cautiously into the depths of the cavern. All around them, it was evident that most of the cave's size had recently been excavated by machinery. Dozens of steel beams welded together were used throughout to reinforce the cave walls and ceiling that seemed to be held up primarily by four larger beams that arched upward and met in the middle.

Sequoia and Mesquite crept down the passageway to the left with the wolf pup in the lead. As they inched along, the sounds of construction got louder and louder — welding, hammering, and riveting of metals, but also the continued excavation of the cave itself. Drilling and scraping sounds were booming off the walls and the ground beneath their feet shook and vibrated. Machinery, hydraulics and vehicles could also be heard. Occasional voices from the Soldierjacks would mix with the rest of the discord, but so far the wolf and the bear didn't detect anything human at all.

Their passageway ultimately spilled out into the main cavern. The twosome snuck out into the vast underground dome and hid behind one of the unmanned computer terminals. They could see the Copterjet parked in the center and the massive doors behind it that let it in. All around them, Soldierjacks worked tirelessly as they focused on their mission of making the site fully operational.

Meanwhile, Cedar and the girls snuck down their chosen corridor, ever alert for footsteps or voices or any sign of trouble. After quite a ways, it eventually led into a large room filled with an enormous machine and dozens of Soldierjacks busily working on it.

The octagon-shaped contraption in the center of the room was the size of eight full-sized cars standing on end. It had water and power cables running into it, dials and gauges all over and about a dozen pipes that jutted in and out from it. A conveyor belt of sorts ran into it from somewhere down another corridor on the opposite side of the room. One extra-long metal tube extended out from the top, which seemed to go right up into the cavern's roof at a 45-degree angle.

"What do you suppose that is?" Juniper asked her friends, who obviously had no idea either.

"Dunno," Cedar growled, "but it can't be good."

Aspen noticed several of the worker-drones were

gathered around a collection of computers at the front of the device, apparently programming it. "We need to see what's on those screens," she said quietly to Juniper and Cedar.

"And just how do you think we're going to accomplish that?" Cedar asked.

"You seem to forget — I'm a flier and you're a grounder," she said. "We don't think alike and I'm willing to gamble that those robots don't really think at all."

With that, she flapped her little wings and launched into the air as silently as she could. She flew up toward the ceiling, around the edge of the room undetected, and then very carefully and gently landed right on top of the single Soldierjack who was standing behind the others, watching over their shoulders as they entered data into the system.

From her vantage point on top of the robot's helmet, she could see all five computer screens. The Soldierjacks were furiously entering data into the computers at a pace no human could possibly match. Aspen certainly couldn't understand computer code and instead focused her keen eyesight on the images, schematics and titles on the pages popping up on the screens.

After a minute or so, Aspen was able to gather enough information to get an idea what the nearly assembled machine was being built for. She turned to

her two friends hiding in the corner and, unable to contain herself, burst out loud with excitement from her perch on the Soldierjack's head, "It's a capacitor! It's a toxic capacitor called a Phoenix!"

Upon hearing a bird cry out, every Soldierjack in the room turned to look at Aspen, still perched on top of the Soldierjack's helmet, who realized she had just blown her cover.

Across the cavern complex, Mesquite and Sequoia were still looking for clues and trying to find the man in charge of the whole operation.

They dashed from hiding place to hiding place, hustling their way to the tunnel on the other side that they hadn't been down yet. Working as a team, they managed to scoot behind moving forklifts, stationary objects and steel beams until they reached the opposite wall without being spotted.

Panting, Sequoia turned to Mesquite. "Can you sm-sm-smell that?" the little bear asked. "There's something human down this h-h-hallway, but the scent's not right...."

"I can hear him, too — he breathes funny, like he's wearing a gas mask or something," Mesquite added.

After making sure the way was clear, they darted down the corridor to the next room.

It was the lab. Inside, they could see a small man with a large moustache and horribly discolored skin leaning over a microscope. He was wearing a lab coat and was intently working on something. His mouth

seemed to be permanently attached to a breathing apparatus with two long black tubes that connected to what looked like a giant man-made spider.

Mesquite and Sequoia looked on in awe at the enormous artificial metal insect. It had a computer for its face and big tubes filled with weird chemicals and pumping machines attached on its back that seemed to be recirculating the scientist's air.

Mesquite looked at Sequoia. "That has got to be Doctor Kaustik!"

Suddenly the SPIDER reacted as if it had heard Mesquite's whisper. It rose higher on its legs and turned to scan the room with a red beam of light.

Immediately, Mesquite and Sequoia withdrew from the room and clung to the wall outside. They tried to control their breathing, but the panic of being detected was intense.

Dr. Kaustik looked up from his microscope. "What do you see? Who's there?" he asked his mechanical monster, knowing full well it didn't speak.

After three seconds that seemed to last three minutes, the computer monitor on the SPIDER's face flickered and a pop-up window appeared on it. "Incoming transmission from Mr. Nathan Axxes," it read and in a split second the screen opened wider to show a live video feed from Nathan's office.

Dr. Kaustik called his SPIDER back and it swiveled immediately so the doctor could see the computer screen again.

"Kaustik, this is Axxes," the operation's overlord said. "Give me a status report."

"Mr. Axxes, all is well," the Mongolian scientist reported. "The capacitor is nearly complete. My latest samples of the air contaminant show 100% absorption potential. You should be hearing reports of difficulty breathing in three states in five days or less and two or three other targeted states by month's end."

The doctor continued, "Two small issues came up, both of which I took care of: a malfunctioning Soldier-jack that I dealt with personally, and, on my flight out here a couple hours ago, some idiot photographers in a hot air balloon were getting a little close so I made sure they had a little accident."

Nathan Axxes leaned in closer to the digital video camera connected to his office computer. "What do you mean by 'little accident?'"

Kaustik, as proud as ever, grinned from behind his mouthpiece and told his boss exactly what had happened. "I flew the Copterjet into their airspace and collapsed their canopy. Last I saw of them, they were crashing into the Grand Canyon."

From just outside the lab, Sequoia and Mesquite

overheard everything. They were shocked at the heartless deeds being committed, but held back from doing anything foolish. They wanted to bring this info back to the whole team.

"My dear doctor," Axxes replied, his words ripe with warning and frustration, "you had better make sure those people did not survive. Send a Soldierjack squad out to confirm it. We cannot have any mistakes and we cannot draw any attention to ourselves. Do I make myself clear?"

Dr. Kaustik, expecting praise for his actions instead of orders and threats, woefully replied, "Perfectly clear, Mr. Axxes. Perfectly."

In the other room, all the way across the expanse of the underground chamber, Aspen knew she was in deep trouble.

She jumped off the helmet of the Soldierjack she was balancing on, spread her wings and swooped down to where Cedar and Juniper awaited in the corner.

In mid-flight, a Soldierjack moved to intercept her. She swerved and corrected her course to avoid being caught, only to draw the attention of two others. They raised their hands to catch her, but at the last second she managed to pull up and escape their reach by skimming across the roof and landing on one of the support beams. She was already pretty tired. Every Soldierjack in the room was focused on the little bird with the turquoise amulet hanging from its neck.

Aspen's teammates decided to cause a diversion and rescue their friend. Cedar ran over to the closest computer main power cable, clenched it in his teeth, pulled backward and unplugged it. Juniper jumped up on a chair, then onto the terminal desk and started pushing computer disks, papers and anything small

enough off onto the floor.

The commotion caused the Soldierjacks to turn around. "Zzt! More animals! Remove them!"

Their small size and quickness proved a challenge for the robot workers. The Soldierjacks soon realized they would need their weapons to be rid of these pests in quick order.

As if with a single mind, half of the machine-men turned around and retrieved their Flamesaws stacked in a neat line along one of the walls. With their blades buzzing and the flamethrowers charged, they rushed back in the room to rid themselves of these three pesky trespassers.

Meanwhile, Mesquite and Sequoia had hightailed it away from the lab. They had to find the others, share the evil plans of Axxes, stop the Soldierjack team from locating the humans they had just rescued from the hot-air balloon and somehow stop the capacitor from ever being operational.

They rushed headlong down the corridor, no longer caring if they were seen. A pair of Soldierjacks carrying a heavy generator from each end was directly in their path. Each group spotted the other at exactly the same time.

"Zzt! Intruders! Stop where you are!" the worker drones loudly ordered.

The pup and the cub didn't hesitate — they kept running at full speed right under the generator.

Realizing what the two animals were doing, the Soldierjacks transmitted to each other that they should drop the generator just as they animals ran under it. Each robot let go and the heavy machine crashed to the floor with a loud, crunching sound.

"Good thing we stopped when we did!" Mesquite wisecracked.

"G-g-got that right, buddy!" Sequoia added.

The Soldierjacks looked at the two infant animals that had slid to a stop an inch before actually going under the generator. Then they looked down to realize they had just dropped the generator on their own feet, crushing them painlessly but completely.

Mesquite and Sequoia giggled, jumped up on the generator, over to the other side of it and continued running down the hallway.

Back in the capacitor room, Cedar, Juniper and Aspen knew they needed to get away. Even if they transformed, the room was too tight to offer much room to battle and the Soldierjacks with their flamethrowers would have the upper hand.

"Let's get out of here!" Juniper yelled as she leaped off the computer terminal and scrambled for the door with Cedar in close pursuit behind her.

Aspen saw her chance and took to wing, soaring down and toward the exit. She watched her two partners squeeze under the legs of a Soldierjack and escape down the passageway.

That's when a fiery blast from one of the androids filled the doorway and scorched the edge of her left wing. Aspen screamed and turned, her wobbly flight taking her to the conveyor belt where she crash-landed.

Her friends in the hall turned just in time to see it all take place. Two Soldierjacks blocked the doorway, brandishing their Flamesaws with deadly intent.

Aspen looked around desperately for a way to escape and finally found one. Up past the conveyor belt and inside the capacitor itself, she spotted a circular beam of sunlight. The tube! The metal tube that exits from the top of the machine leads up and outside!

Aspen shouted to her friends in the hall, "Guys, I'll meet you and the others outside! I'll fly out the other end of this pipe! Now go before they catch you!"

Just as a Soldierjack swiped at her with the spinning blade of his Flamesaw, Aspen hopped up and managed to fly as best she could into the machine and up into the pipe.

She could see the sunlight far up ahead and even smell the fresh air coming from the opening nearly a half-mile away at the other end. With sheer determination,

she made for the outlet.

SJ-One had arrived on scene to witness Aspen's escape. He immediately took control. "Zzt! Close the extraction tube end caps! Seal it on both sides!"

Another drone tapped a couple keys and it was done. Remotely controlled covers slid into place in the long pipe leading to the surface. Aspen, halfway up the tube, was stuck.

Inside the tube, the peregrine falcon youngling saw the sun go out in front of her as the end cap locked into place. Then the light from the room to her backside went dark and she knew she was trapped.

She also knew she couldn't use her super-powers inside the metal pipe — it was too small and she would be crushed if she grew any larger at all. Her only hope now lay in the hands of her friends.

Mesquite and Sequoia had made their way to the storage room where they stopped to catch their breath and meet up with the other team. Sequoia watched from the entrance to see if the others were on their way while Mesquite quickly scouted the room.

In no time, Cedar and Juniper came barreling down the hall and into the storage room.

"We gotta go, now!" Cedar demanded.

"Where's Aspen? She's supposed to be with you!" Mesquite said.

"She found another way out. We need to leave now!" Juniper cut in.

They could hear the stomping footsteps of Soldierjacks running down the hall. They had twenty seconds at best.

Mesquite had an idea. "Quick! Everyone! We gotta drag this rabbit cage over to the door and open it up. These guys will give us some extra time to get out!"

The foursome ran over to the wire cage crammed with eager-to-escape rabbits and shoved it into the corridor. Just as a dozen fully armed Soldierjacks turned the corner, Mesquite sprung the bolt and pulled the door open.

Immediately the bunnies leaped out of their wire prison and zipped around the hallway, hopping back and forth in a frenzy.

Some of the Soldierjacks in front tripped over the spastic rabbits and fell face first, smashing their faceplates on the floor while their weapons clattered against the ground. More of the Axxes androids tumbled to the ground when they tripped over the Soldierjacks who fell before them.

By the time the rabbits hopped off out of sight inside the cave somewhere, only seven Soldierjacks remained standing. All seven leveled their Flamesaws at the Natural Forces animals fleeing down the corridor

to the back door. They fired, but the firestorm wasn't quite close enough to do any damage.

At the rear entry, the animals slid to a stop in front of the steel door.

"Open it! Open it!" Juniper screamed, knowing the Soldierjacks would fry them where they stood if they couldn't get the door open.

Sequoia and Mesquite pushed on it as hard as they could while Cedar scratched away with his tiny badger nails, but it wasn't budging.

Juniper turned to see the door had a keypad next to it at human-hand level. It had a green arrow pointing up and a red arrow pointing down. It was obvious what she had to do.

"Guys! The keypad! We have to hit the green button!" she screamed as she pointed to their salvation.

"It's too tall!" Cedar yelled.

"Stack up! Sequoia, let Mesquite get on your back! I'll climb up!"

They did as she suggested and the little black-footed ferret scampered up her grizzly and wolf pals until, by stretching with all her might, she managed to reach up and tap the green arrow.

The door shot open, sliding into the mountainside.

Just as the Soldierjacks got within reach, the hasty mammal pyramid broke apart and the four critters

scrambled out into the sun and ran away down the trail.

The Soldierjacks stopped at the back door, their speaker-boxes crackling in unison, "Zzt! Area secure. Animals evicted."

Mesquite, Sequoia, Cedar and Juniper finally stopped running about 300 yards from the cave. They were exhausted. The foursome took refuge in a spot far enough down the trail that they had time to react if any Soldierjacks were sent after them. They also wanted to make sure they could be spotted by Aspen from above as they expected her arrival any second.

"So what did you guys find out?" Mesquite asked Cedar and Juniper with his eyes focused tightly on the trailhead.

"Well," the badger said, "Aspen looked at their computers and found out they're building a machine that shoots some sort of poison in the air so the humans breathe it."

"She should be here any minute now. That tube she flew up into can't be that long," Juniper said.

Mesquite and the others turned their eyes to the sky above the cave complex in hopes of spotting their little feathered friend. "Sequoia and I saw Dr. Kaustik," Mesquite reported. "He's trouble. We overheard him talking to his boss, Mr. Axxes. This capacitor thing

they are making is almost complete. It has some sort of dust that will make it hard for people to breathe. I don't even want to think about what it will do to the animals."

"And he has a giant r-r-robot spider," Sequoia added. "Axxes told that crazy doctor to send out some Soldierjacks t-t-to make sure those humans in the balloon we rescued didn't survive the f-f-fall."

"We have to stop this," Juniper pleaded. "These guys are evil."

Cedar growled. "I can't wait to sink my claws into 'em!"

"We have to wait for Aspen," Mesquite said. "Where is she? What's taking her so long?"

Inside the cave, Dr. Kaustik was demanding a report from SJ-One who was wirelessly gathering information from all the Soldierjacks' memory banks and visual data logs. In less than two minutes, he had collected and translated the data and was ready to report.

"Zzt! Doctor Kaustik, it appears that a group of young animals not native to this area and wearing strange necklaces somehow broke into the facility," he reported. "They caused some disruption, but no real damage. They escaped out the back door. I estimate time loss of 9.5 minutes. However, the rabbits all got loose and it will take some extra time to recapture all of them."

The doctor was baffled. "Animals? Why, how…"

"Zzt! Sir, we captured one of them. A bird. Falcon species, possibly peregrine. It is still in the extraction tube," SJ-One continued.

"Excellent, SJ-One." the doctor retorted. "Keep it in there. Let's test how well that little creature can handle our first full strength test-fire of the capacitor! We'll roast its little lungs!

"And don't worry about the rabbits. If the animals went out the back door as you say then I'm sure the snake made a meal for himself. Just get us back on track," the doctor said to his favored robot worker. Kaustik made sure that all new upgrades and the best equipment went into SJ-One, the most advanced of all the drones. If the SPIDER was the doctor's caretaker and protector, then SJ-One was his best friend. "I want this capacitor to be functional as soon as possible, Number One."

"Zzt! Yes, sir," SJ-One replied.

"Oh, and send out a squad to confirm those balloonists didn't survive," Kaustik added. "Make sure they're well equipped, too. If they encounter any more pesky stray animals, I want them dealt with permanently."

"Zzt. Consider it done, Doctor Kaustic," his android supervisor said.

Back on the trailhead, the four little mammals were

growing impatient waiting for their feathered friend.

"Something's wrong. Aspen should have gotten out by now," Cedar said, concerned.

"I hope she wasn't captured," Juniper said quietly. "Or worse…"

Suddenly, Mesquite spotted a crew of Soldierjacks marching down the path. Each was carrying advanced Axxes-designed equipment that doubled as deadly weapons if used in a hostile manner: Nailguns, Chainsaws, Trenchguns. They were headed quickly down the trail toward the animal kids who were still waiting for their last member to arrive.

"That must be the squad they're sending out to find the humans we saved," Mesquite said with a snarl.

"We gotta do s-s-something," Sequoia pleaded.

Mesquite looked at the team. He knew they were running out of options. It was time to act.

CHAPTER 11

"Let's do it!" Mesquite shouted.

Bright blue shards of light erupted around the four animals as they shape-shifted, each in a whirlwind of Arizona dust, ancient magic and mystical energy. In a matter of seconds, all four creatures had transformed into their humanoid alter-egos and poised ready to save their friend and take down the evil forces in front of them.

Mesquite leaped up onto a rocky ledge for a better view and a more tactical position. He pointed with his turquoise-tipped lance that always appeared whenever he morphed toward the oncoming squad of Soldierjacks. "Juniper! You need to get to the top of this mountain to rescue Aspen. Tear that pipe open if you have to! Sequoia! Can you throw her that far?"

Sequoia, now an absolutely massive bipedal grizzly rippling with muscle under his thick fur, looked up at the craggy cliff face above the cave entrance. It was a long half-mile to the top. "Jump into my hand, Juniper! You're going for a ride!"

Juniper didn't hesitate. Once transformed, she was

particularly spry and she sprang off a nearby rock and landed with hardly a sound in Sequoia's huge mitt before the bear could even blink. "Let's do this, big guy!" she exclaimed.

Meanwhile, super-powered Cedar energized his claws and soon they were like glowing sapphires. He bared his fangs at the approaching enemy and cranked his head to the left and then to the right, his neck bones crackling with tension. Cedar was ready and eager for a fight. Not waiting a second longer, he tore into the surface and started tunneling underground with amazing speed toward the oncoming Soldierjacks.

Sequoia shifted his sizable weight and lowered his right arm that held Juniper nearly to the ground. He aimed toward the top of the ridge with his magical shield that was wrapped around his left arm. Juniper readied herself and crouched in his powerful hand, prepared to launch. Then, with his teeth clenched, Sequoia tensed and with a loud roar, pitched the ferret-woman like a catapult.

Juniper rocketed into the sky, shooting over the Soldierjacks who barely had time to respond. She flew up and up toward the top of the mountain. As her momentum slowed, Juniper angled her course and used her speed to ricochet off the cliff walls, springboarding from one ledge to another and, like a pinball,

made it up the last few hundred yards to the top on her own.

Down below, the robots hardly had time to react to all the animal warriors' actions. They broke their marching formation into two lines of five each. The first line of Soldierjacks kneeled down and leveled their Flamesaws at Mesquite and Sequoia who were not far away up the path, almost within range of the flamethrowers. Two of the Soldierjacks in the second line were carrying amplified, high-powered, belt-fed Nailguns while the other three all held brutally powerful Trenchguns that fired a forceful blast used primarily to dig ditches up to three feet deep in solid rock.

Fearless, Mesquite jumped off the ledge he was perched on and landed directly into the Soldierjacks' path. A smile curiously slid across his wolfen face as he stood his ground just a few feet in front of the formidable regiment.

Just as the Soldierjacks were about to open fire on the man-wolf with a fatal blast of flames, the ground in front of them exploded open and Cedar burst out. With his claws gleaming, he slashed right through the Flamesaws in front of him that were aimed at Mesquite.

Chaos filled the startled Soldierjack ranks as the robots fell clumsily back and out of formation.

Mesquite ran forward. Using his spear as a pole vault, he leaped over Cedar and directly into the enemy squad. With smashing blows and fierce kicks, he managed to topple several of them before he brought his spear around and rammed it directly into the chest cavity of the nearest Soldierjack. It fell to its knees, convulsed and shut down as electrical sparks started shooting from its lethal wound like a miniature fireworks display.

Sequoia joined the fray and used his powerful fists to hammer one and then two Soldierjacks into worthless metallic heaps. One of the remaining androids brought up his Trenchgun and fired a thunderous blast at the grizzly. Sequoia swung his magical shield in front of him just in time, absorbing the entire discharge harmlessly.

"Oh no, you don't!" the giant bear bellowed and after two massive steps he was on the villain. With incredible quickness, Sequoia grabbed the Trenchgun, pulled it right out of the Soldierjack's steely grip, and brought it smashing down on the robot's head. The machine-man buckled under the blow and fell onto its back, motionless.

Cedar was a growling tornado of clenched teeth and deadly claws as he tore into what was left of the Soldierjack force. They fell in pieces and parts all around him as his swirling, slashing arms ripped through their

alloy bodies and computerized parts.

In short order, the battle was over. Ten intimidating, million-dollar Soldierjacks lay wasted at the feet of the three animal guardians.

On the ridge high above the cluttered battlefield, Juniper had located the pipe jutting a few inches upward out of the solid stone beneath. She could see the end of it was shut — a mechanical lid had closed and sealed her friend Aspen inside.

Juniper reached over her shoulder and pulled out one of the dozen wooden batons stuffed inside the leather knapsack that appeared out of nowhere on her back whenever she transformed. A radiating turquoise flat blade instantly appeared on its tip, creating a mystical hatchet. Juniper used her hatchets with great skill as cutting, throwing or chopping weapons.

The super-powered ferret sprang upward, her hatchet above her head, and as she came down she swung it with great force onto the pipe's edge. It cleaved right through the metal tube with hardly a sound. The pipe was open again.

Juniper stuck her snout in the pipe and shouted, "Aspen! Are you down there?" She heard her own echo but that was all.

For a few moments, there was silence. Then, from deep within, she heard Aspen shout. "Juniper! I'm coming out!"

Aspen pushed with all her might upward to the open end of the pipe. She hardly had room to flap her wings; it was mostly all clawing away at the smooth, steel sides with her talons. After a few minutes, she could see Juniper's black hand reaching down inside to help her out. Aspen gave one final push and grasped Juniper's outstretched fingers with her wing. In less than a second, her dear ferret friend plucked her out of the tight tube and into the fresh air.

"You saved me!" Aspen said as she coughed and collapsed to the rocky surface, trying to catch her breath. "Thank you! I wasn't sure I'd ever see the sun again."

"We're sisters, Aspen," Juniper replied. "We weren't going to leave you."

"How are the others?" she asked after a brief pause.

"Just fine. Sounds to me like they just took out the trash down there," the ferret said with a smile.

One hundred yards in front of Mesquite, Cedar and Sequoia, the cave's back door unexpectedly slid open. Out from the shadows stepped Doctor Kaustik flanked by SJ-One and followed by the SPIDER.

"Very intriguing," the vile doctor said as he looked at the three heroes in their power forms. "I don't know what you are exactly or even why you're here, but this is your last day on earth. I am going to enjoy dissecting all of you, vermin," the doctor threatened, his voice

rasping through the voice transmitter in his breathing apparatus.

The animal adventurers bared their teeth at their foe. They crouched and readied for his attack.

Kaustik turned to his SPIDER, unhooked himself from it and set it loose. Simultaneously, SJ-One stepped forward and revealed that he was wielding a Rivet Rifle — a heavy-duty tool used by Axxes Construction to fire red-hot rivets into steel beams. It required its user to be harnessed into a whole system; a small thermo-nuclear engine was carried in a large backpack while the rivets were force-fed at a high rate through it, superheated, and shot with great force out a long bar-rel like a futuristic musket.

The SPIDER skittered forward aggressively and leaped up on the boulders in between the back door and the heroes, its legs spread across both sides of the trail.

SJ-One fired his first volley of rivets. They streaked at Mesquite like glowing orange missiles.

Mesquite dodged the stream of molten projectiles and spun himself over behind Sequoia, who hoisted up his supernatural shield. The barrage of sizzling rivets slammed against his shield and fell to the ground where they cooked the sand around them.

Cedar hurdled into action, launching himself at full

speed at the SPIDER squatting menacingly on the boulders. With claws extended, the badger lurched at the mechanical monster. It flung itself to the side, dodging Cedar's attack, and slammed one of its hardened alloy legs against its opponent.

Cedar crashed to the rocky ground, rolled and turned to face the giant six-legged beast.

"You're quicker than I thought, monster!" Cedar yelled at it, hiding the pain he was feeling. "But you're going to lose. I'm gonna carve you wide open!"

Mesquite jumped out from the safety of Sequoia's shield and raised his spear into a throwing position. With fantastic force and speed, he hurled the javelin at SJ-One, who was moving in for a better shot. The spear flew like a torpedo, glanced hard off the weapon in the robot's hands, and knocked it to the dirt.

As SJ-One bent down to pick it back up, Mesquite moved in. Sprinting in at full speed, the half-wolf, half-man jumped up and on his way down bashed his big fists against the back of the android's head. The impact flattened SJ-One against the ground.

The SPIDER was monitoring the entire battle with its multiple camera-eyes. Realizing its partner was down, it altered its tactics. Swiveling its body, the SPIDER opened a receptacle in its backside and fired a strand of electro-magnetic cable at Cedar. The metal

coils instantly wrapped around the unsuspecting man-sized badger. In seconds, he was almost completely encased by the cable. Then the SPIDER sent a powerful electrical charge down the line, zapping Cedar with a massive shower of volts. Cedar collapsed unconscious to the ground.

Sequoia was already moving in to help while all this was going on. The big bear bounded over to the SPIDER with one massive fist raised high in the air.

Detecting the pending assault by the big bear, the metal arachnid swung around and pointed its nozzles at the grizzly. Sequoia raised his shield again just in time as the deadly spray of acid blasted against his spiritually forged shield. The volatile liquid dripped off harmlessly to the earth.

Unstoppable, Sequoia charged shield first into the SPIDER. He hit it hard — hard enough to knock it back and cause it to lose its balance. A horrendous "clang!" boomed out across the canyon.

The SPIDER recovered quickly and scurried thirty feet up the side of the cliff wall, dragging Cedar, who was still trapped in its cable, behind it. It turned, hanging nearly vertical from the steep rocks, and fired another stream of erosive liquid at Sequoia. The bear managed to protect himself again with his shield in the nick of time.

Far above the fight, Juniper peered over the edge of the cliff. She could barely see her friends battling below. She turned to Aspen who was trying to get her bearings.

"We need to get down there to help, Aspen!" Juniper exclaimed. "How soon can you morph and fly us down there?"

Aspen raised her head. "Give me a minute, Juniper. I just need a minute."

Mesquite saw that his friends had their hands full with the giant robot-spider. He left SJ-One, who was still flat on the ground, and went to recover his trusty spear that was at the base of the ridge the SPIDER had clamored up.

Sequoia grew enraged. He turned to notice a huge rock was next to him. With almost no effort, he picked it up.

"I certainly don't need my fists to smash you to smithereens!" the bear roared at the SPIDER as he hoisted the small boulder over his head.

Mesquite looked over to see his friend getting ready to hurl the heavy stone. "Sequoia, wait…!" Mesquite yelled, but it was too late.

Sequoia heaved the giant rock at the SPIDER who compressed its legs and skittered sideways across the stony cliff. The boulder smashed against the

mountainside, exactly where the SPIDER had just been. The impact caused a massive shower of rocks to fall directly on top of Mesquite, who was scrambling to get out of the way. He wasn't fast enough. The avalanche collapsed all around him, burying him alive beneath four tons of shattered mountainside.

Digging its tapered metal legs into the rock, the SPIDER hurried across the cliff face with Cedar helplessly trailing along behind it. Then it suddenly came to a stop.

As Cedar's body swung directly below it like a pendulum, the SPIDER cut its cord. Cedar, wrapped like a mummy in the tight metal bindings, tumbled off the ledge and down across the trail to the other side. He bounded and crashed uncontrollably down the embankment, forty feet below to the river rapids.

SJ-One stood up and, with his Rivet Rifle again in his arms, scanned the area. He focused on the only remaining combatant in view, took aim, and discharged a salvo of super-heated rivets at the man-grizzly.

Sequoia leaped over the edge of the trail just as a hailstorm of hot mushroom-shaped iron projectiles streaked past his head. The fight would have to wait. He had to save Cedar, who was being washed downstream under the hammering waters of the Colorado River.

With the enemy defeated, Dr. Kaustik recalled his SPIDER and SJ-One. After reconnecting to his six-legged caretaker, he led his team back inside the cave's rear door. Time was of the essence.

The toxic scientist was all too pleased at the performance of his machines. "Well done, boys!" the doctor said. "Now seal this back door permanently and post some guards just in case. This is the last I want to see of those creatures!"

"Aspen! They need us!" Juniper shouted. She had witnessed the end of the fight from her vantage point. "You've got to try!"

Aspen rolled over and stood up on her little falcon legs. They were a bit shaky. She shook off her exhaustion. "Alright. I can do this!"

She inhaled deeply and summoned her metamorphosis. Her amulet grew brighter and brighter until it seemed a blue-green sun erupted from it. Beams of light broke out all around her as the pint-sized falcon chick merged into the spirit of a Native American warrior. In an instant it was complete.

Juniper couldn't wait. Excited and fully aware of her friends in peril, she leaped off the cliff fearlessly. She straightened out her long body and shot toward the ground like an arrow.

Aspen took three steps toward the edge and dove off after her. Tucking her wings back and pointing her beak, the super-sized, super-powered peregrine falcon raced like lightning after Juniper. In the blink of an eye she had caught up to her, grabbed her in her talons

and continued streaking toward the earth's surface.

Meanwhile, Sequoia reached the river's edge in a controlled but messy skid. Rocks and soil flew all around him as he hit solid ground with a loud thud next to the fast-flowing waters.

"Cedar!" the bear yelled, hoping his friend was conscious and could hear him. "Where are you?!" The big bear hustled as best he could along the waterway trying to spot his friend being swept away.

Downstream a ways, the badger had roused from his electrocution. Cedar was violently bobbing up and down in the river, slamming against giant moss-covered rocks in the waterway. The SPIDER's cable had pinned his arms against his sides — he couldn't get his claws out to cut through them. It was all he could do to stay afloat and not inhale gallons of water by keeping his head up.

He thought he heard Sequoia yelling but the rapids were too loud. He couldn't be sure. Then something caught his eye. A strange but familiar shadow zoomed across the sun overhead and swooped down at him. It was Aspen, and she was carrying Juniper!

The falcon honed in on her friend fighting for survival in the river. She pitched downward, opened her talons and released Juniper who landed perfectly on Cedar's wire-wrapped chest.

Clinging to him with one hand, she pulled out one of her hatchets and with a quick swipe, cut him loose. Without missing a beat, she turned, lunged off him and sprang to a boulder sticking up out of the water.

Aspen circled around and dove down again.

"Cedar! Grab my foot as I come by!" she screamed above the sound of the rushing river.

The badger shed himself of the last of the coils and reached up with his hand just as Aspen sped by. Like a vise, she grabbed onto her friend's outstretched fist. With extra strong strokes of her wings, she dragged the half-drowned badger-warrior to shore and set down next to him.

Juniper leaped from the boulder she was on to a smaller one and then landed next to Cedar, who was coughing up river water. He looked beat but angry.

Soon Sequoia rushed up to them as well. "Thought we lost ya, Cedar!" the bear exclaimed. Then he looked at his female friends. "Sure glad you two showed up!"

"Where's Mesquite?" Juniper asked.

Sequoia's face turned somber. "He was caught in an avalanche during the battle. I'm not sure he made it."

Without a word, Aspen took off like a rocket, soaring straight up and back upriver to find Mesquite.

Juniper looked up at Sequoia. "I'll stay here with Cedar. We're going to need your muscle to move those

rocks. Go! Save Mesquite!"

The bear turned and ran off to rescue his pal.

Cedar, still on his hands and knees, shook himself like a wet dog. "I'll be alright, Juniper. Thanks for saving me back there." He coughed and faltered a little as he tried to stand. "I hope Mesquite's okay. It's going to take all five of us to bring these guys down."

Back at the rock pile, Aspen was frantically calling for her friend buried somewhere inside when Sequoia showed up.

"I'm here!" Mesquite finally groaned from deep within the rubble. "Get these rocks off me!"

Sequoia started tossing rocks like they were pillows. In a short while, he pulled Mesquite free from his stone-covered grave. The wolf was covered in stones, dust and dirt but he had survived the accident with deep bruises and more than a few bumps, but no broken bones.

"Thanks, Sequoia," Mesquite said after spitting some pebbles out of his mouth. "You gotta control that temper of yours," he added with a grin.

Juniper and Cedar crawled up over the trail's edge to rejoin the others.

"You alright?" the badger asked.

"Yeah. Thanks," Mesquite said. "You don't look so good yourself."

The badger couldn't hide his anger. "Good enough for a second round. That spider's mine!"

"What do you want to do now, Mesquite?" Aspen asked, hoping he was healthy enough but also for a plan that would settle the score.

Mesquite paused for a second and then looked at Juniper. "The back door's certainly no longer an option. Do you think you could find where the aircraft entered this secret base?"

"Sure," she replied. "I know exactly where it is."

Mesquite turned briefly back to the rock pile that had nearly crushed him, pulled his spear out from under it, straightened up and then wiped a layer of red dust off his leg with his free hand. "Then how about we go knock on the front door?" he said with a bitter smile on his face and a clever plan in his head.

CHAPTER
13

The sun was getting close to setting and the canyon reflected this fact by casting a burnt-orange, dark gold and brick-red hue to everything within it. The clouds on the horizon seemed almost painted with autumn colors and as the temperature dropped, so too did the shadows grow longer.

From out of the setting sun a silhouette appeared. It was Aspen, still in her heroine role, clutching a small shape in each claw. At high speed, she soared down directly at the rocky ridge — aimed right at the well-concealed bay doors to the secret lair of Axxes.

When she got close, she pulled up sharply and dropped the thing in her left talon. The peculiar pack-age fell freely at first, but then erupted in a bath of teal-colored cosmic light. From within the neon-blue ball of energy a much larger shape formed and fell through the air. It was Cedar, his claws radiating brightly with the same energy that transformed him. Claws first, he impacted hard into the giant hidden hangar doors.

His nails punched ten holes through the false outer

rocky covering and the steel doors behind it as well. Then gravity took over. With his claws still punctured through the bay doors he slid downward, ripping huge tears in the disguised gateway all the way down to the bottom like ten knives cutting through cloth.

Now it was Sequoia's turn. Aspen dive-bombed and dropped him next, still in his young form and, just like Cedar, he morphed while falling through the air.

With the doors weakened by Cedar's shredding assault, the giant-sized, fully powered grizzly angled himself so he would hit them with full force, shield first.

A deafening explosion filled the cavern as Sequoia crashed through the hangar doors, spraying steel shrapnel all across the cave. He rolled as he landed with a loud thump and skidded to a halt just in front of the Copterjet, one hand grasping his shield, the other clenched in a fist. With a wide grin on his face, he rose up, ready for action.

The Soldierjacks were all caught unaware. Intruder alarms went off, lights flashing, sirens wailing, and soon the whole complex was alerted to the invasion. Robot drones stopped working and scrambled for their weapons.

By then, the rest of the Natural Forces had entered through the bay doors that Sequoia and Cedar had torn open. They were itching for a fight.

Aspen struck first. She was circling the cavern from an elevated position, quietly and gracefully soaring along its roof, with a perfect view of the entire place. As the first Soldierjacks ran forward to engage the animal invaders, she paused in mid-flight and whipped her wings in a downward slashing motion. A dozen supercharged, turquoise feathers streaked out from their host and tore into the robots' chest cavities like explosive arrows. Her wings instantaneously replaced the missing feathers with new ones and she swooped around to fire another salvo.

Mesquite moved in on the offensive. He ran and leaped directly into a squad of metal-men with his spear at the ready. Ramming the lance straight through one Soldierjack's head, he nearly knocked it off, sending electrical sparks spitting in all directions. Another android swiped at him with his Flamesaw's carving blade but Mesquite ducked, knocked the robot off his feet with a spinning kick, and put it out of commission with an elbow smash to the faceplate.

Two other Soldierjacks moved in with high-powered Nailguns. They positioned themselves on each side of Mesquite and fired. The man-wolf was too clever and too fast. He leaped straight up in the air with his powerful legs as the bullet-like nails missed their intended target, and instead they shot each other. With fifty

nails embedded deep into each of their bodies, they fell forward with a heavy crash, permanently disabled.

Mesquite landed in a fighting stance. With furious fists, brutal kicks and one last stab with his spear, three more Soldierjacks toppled.

Juniper didn't delay and took off at high speed, holding one of her mystical hatchets in each hand. She rocketed herself into a threesome of the robots who fired flaming bursts at her with their Flamesaws, but she was faster than they could aim.

Amongst the blazing bright orange barrages, she maneuvered around her opponents. She started with slashing blows at their knees and as they fell, she finished them off with fast chops until they stopped moving.

Sequoia moved out from behind the Copterjet and starting bashing Soldierjacks with his huge fists. When he wasn't using his shield to protect himself from flying nails and flamethrowers, he used it as a weapon and sent robots flying across the cavern from the force of the blow it produced with the mighty grizzly swinging it.

Cedar was in the midst of the brawl as well, grinning ear to ear. The super-powered badger preferred to fight with ferocity, up close and personal. His claws carved up, down, across and straight through a bevy of

Soldierjacks as he literally tore through the robotic Axxes army.

For a few minutes, the cavern blared with the sounds of battle. Bangs, blasts and bursts echoed off the walls until finally it fell silent as the last of the Soldierjack troopers fell to its knees and then on its face after Cedar ripped out a handful of computer components from its chest.

Breathing heavily, the five heroes looked at each other approvingly as they moved back together to regroup. They had taken care of the henchmen. Now they were ready for the big boys.

As if on cue, Dr. Kaustik strode out into the cavern with his SPIDER behind him and SJ-One at his side. He was furious. In front of him lay dozens of his Soldierjack robot workers, torn apart and smashed beyond repair. This mysterious force of five animals had destroyed his warrior workforce and put the entire operation in jeopardy. He planned to deal with them most harshly.

While the doctor hurriedly turned to disconnect from his SPIDER and turn it loose on his enemies with a vengeance, SJ-One stepped forward carrying a Trench-gun in each hand.

Mesquite eyed his opponents. Five against two, but the SPIDER had proven itself earlier and the Soldierjack commander was no slouch either. "Stick to

the plan, everyone," Mesquite loudly ordered his team-mates. "Watch yourselves with that spider-bot — he's faster than you think. I'll take on the guy with the guns. Spread out and shut these machines down!"

A rather evil-looking smile slithered across Cedar's face as he stared at Kaustik's six-legged servant. "You should have finished me when you had the chance, creature," he growled. "It's payback time!"

"Destroy them!" Dr. Kaustik screamed to his last, but best, robots. "Tear them to shreds!"

The SPIDER skittered across the cave floor and then leaped into the midst of the Natural Forces team. The animals scattered out of its way and clear of its giant dagger-like legs.

As soon as it landed, the SPIDER's sharpened limbs stabbed into the steel floor. Six loud steel-on-steel, ear-piercing "clang" sounds rang out simultaneously.

The SPIDER swung its head around and fired a blast of its toxic venom at Cedar, who was moving in for an attack. The badger barely dodged the deadly liquid by diving behind a pile of busted Soldierjacks.

Aspen, circling above, dived down and let loose a barrage of her exploding feathers. The missiles detonated against the alloy body of the SPIDER in a shower of turquoise but with little effect.

Juniper took off at high speed, pulled a hatchet

from her satchel and zoomed in underneath the dangerous legs of the monster. As she dashed below the beast, she reached up and cut a three-foot-long slice in its weaker underbelly, but the monster was hardly fazed.

The SPIDER spun around and shot its coil at the fast-moving ferret. The silvery cable shot out at incredible speed but Juniper was just too fast. She turned and darted as the steely rope clattered harmlessly against the cave floor. The SPIDER instantly retracted the coil with nothing caught in its grip this time.

Sequoia found an opening and moved in on the SPIDER, his fist high in the air for a hammering blow. But the machine-monster's radar detected his presence and, without even turning its head, it raised two legs and blocked his strike.

Off balance, the bear stumbled behind the SPIDER who shifted again and fired another salvo of its erosive manufactured fluid at Cedar, keeping him pinned down and out of the fight.

Across the cave, Mesquite charged at SJ-One who was ready for his attack. As soon as the wolf got close, he started firing away with his Trenchguns. Powerful, sonic blasts screamed across the cavern at Mesquite who was ducking and dodging each one as he moved in ever closer. Behind him, the shots from the guns exploded against the cave's walls.

Mesquite stayed focused on his target, but he knew one hit from a gun blast like these would be the end. He wished he had Sequoia's shield.

"Zzt! Stand down, animal!" SJ-One demanded, his voice box squawking above the firing from his weapons. "You are trespassing on private property and I order you…"

Mesquite launched himself into a high spinning jump, his spear raised above his head. "Oh, give it a rest, you overgrown wind-up toy!" Mesquite shouted down to his opponent while in mid-leap. Then, he whipped his spear with all of his considerable strength. It left Mesquite's arm like a blue-tipped rocket, jamming straight down the barrel of the Trenchgun SJ-One clutched in his right hand.

The spearhead ripped halfway down the steel barrel and lodged itself in the main area above the trigger. Immediately, the Trenchgun began to tremble, smoke and spit sparks.

Shocked at Mesquite's assault, SJ-One dropped the destroyed gun to the floor. In the two seconds it took him to release the weapon, Mesquite was on him.

The wolf-warrior landed feet first into SJ-One's chest and sent him sprawling. The concussion from the flying drop-kick caused the leader of the robot workers to drop his other Trenchgun, which clattered against

the floor and smashed against cave wall.

Mesquite landed on all fours and jumped again at SJ-One. The cyborg rolled and brought up a brutal kick of his own hard into Mesquite's gut. The wolf buckled over, managed to recover and stay on his feet, but kept one hand on his sore stomach. He was in pain.

"You're better than I thought, robot," Mesquite winced.

SJ-One rose up and ran over to a nearby Soldierjack that the animals had demolished earlier. He pulled the still-functioning Flamesaw from the listless arm of its former user and swung it around toward Mesquite.

But the wolf had pursued SJ-One closely and was right behind him. Just as the weapon came around, Mesquite reached out and stopped it with his hands before it was pointed directly at him. With a sweeping move of his right foot, Mesquite kicked the legs out from under his opponent. SJ-One crashed to the floor on his back, the Flamesaw still pointing upward and still lodged in Mesquite's grip.

Then the warrior-wolf put one foot under SJ-One's jaw, shoving his head back and away. As soon as the robot's grasp on the Flamesaw loosened, Mesquite rammed it down hard and up into the android's metal torso.

The spinning chainsaw blade ripped into SJ-One's midsection, nearly cutting him in two. The robot spasmed

and rolled away, trying to regain its composure.

"You're tougher than the rest, I'll give you that," Mesquite said, and then turned to locate his spear.

After a brief pause to reroute its primary circuits, the leader of the drone workforce went back on the offensive, crawling toward Mesquite like some sort of mechanical zombie. SJ-One was going to fight to the finish.

Mesquite heard the crippled robot coming after him. Quickly, he stepped over to retrieve his spear and pulled it clear of the destroyed Trenchgun just as SJ-One moved in for one last effort to attack his foe.

With both hands, Mesquite thrust his lance, its tip glowing bluish-green as if it were radioactive, directly through SJ-One's helmet and then yanked it back out just as violently. Computer parts, wires and busted pieces of metal scattered across the floor. The robot collapsed in a heap for the final time at Mesquite's feet.

Meanwhile, the SPIDER lurched and discharged its grappling cable at Sequoia. The bear put up his shield to block it, but the coil spun around it and tied itself to Sequoia's large defensive disc as well as his whole left arm.

"Guys! It's got me!" the bear yelled to his teammates just as the SPIDER triggered an electro-blast down the metal line. Sequoia howled in pain and fell to his knees.

Aspen fired another set of her supercharged feathers at the SPIDER, hoping to free her giant friend. They exploded on impact but once more they proved harmless. The SPIDER's armor was heavy-duty indeed.

Juniper — just a turquoise blur — ran in and swiped at the alloy cord tied to Sequoia with her energized hatchets, but the mystical blades glanced off harmlessly. Kaustik had made use of exotic alloy compounds and it would take more than she could dish out to break it.

Another electrocuting shock zipped down the SPIDER's cable and again Sequoia withstood the voltage but roared in agony. The electric shocks the mechanical monster kept sending through the coil were sapping his great strength. He couldn't hang on much longer.

Just then the steel plating in the floor beneath the SPIDER erupted. Cedar had burrowed his way into position and then thrust his way up through the same slit Juniper had ripped open earlier until his deadly claws struck home deep in the SPIDER's underside. Parts of the metal monster spilled out on the floor as if it were being gutted; gears, hoses and steel bracing clattered all around the badger who grinned ear to ear.

"How's that feel, creature?" Cedar snarled.

The SPIDER retreated as best it could. The cable connected to Sequoia fell limp — Cedar's slashes having

cut through the winch inside the machine-monster's body. Two of the SPIDER's legs on its left side seized, forcing it to drag itself away as best it could. Hydraulic fluid dripped from its wound like gushing blood.

But the toxin cannons under its head were still completely functional. The SPIDER swung around and targeted Juniper who had stepped backward toward one of the cave's walls. With its complex infrared and radar tracking systems, it locked onto the ferret who was standing perfectly still, watching the SPIDER's every move. Like high-pressure fire hoses, both barrels fired at Juniper who immediately took off at high speed.

The corrosive spray missed its target and instead splattered against a large steel beam that was directly behind where Juniper had been standing. The liquid ate away at the metal — melting it into a dripping puddle of toxic waste.

Aspen swung around and launched more of her long-range fiery projectiles. This time she aimed for the SPIDER's head and its computerized eyes. Her high-powered feather-arrows hit home in a series of small explosions — one well-placed shot shattering the creature's red-eye targeting system.

The SPIDER rotated its head completely around and fired its nozzles at the peregrine falcon. Aspen dove and turned just in time — and again the SPIDER's

liquid sprayed against a steel structural support beam instead of its desired target. In seconds, the acid corroded through the thick metal, causing a large portion of it to fall to the floor with a horrendous sound that resounded throughout the entire cavern.

Juniper moved in front of the SPIDER and smashed a hatchet into its face. She then flipped backward in a series of somersaults as the wounded robot shot a blast of liquid death at her.

With her amazing speed, Juniper propelled herself out of the way of the lethal stream. As before, it instead showered the third of four primary support beams that arched upward and held up the cave's roof. Like the others, it devoured the steel on contact into a steaming pool of liquid steel.

"Mission accomplished, team! Great job, girls; you got it to melt the cave's support system!" Mesquite screamed to his animal friends. "This whole cave is going to collapse once that last beam gives out. Let's wrap this up!"

"With pleasure!" Sequoia bellowed from next to the Copterjet. The mighty grizzly set down his shield and put his huge mitts on the Axxes aircraft. With one powerful heave, he lifted the entire flying machine off the ground and up over his head. Sequoia had recovered from the SPIDER's electrocutions. He was angry.

The SPIDER slowly dragged itself around in a circle, stabbing blindly away with one of its good legs, hoping to bayonet one of the relentless animal fighters. Visionless, it was having a difficult time locating its animal attackers. The toxic liquid tanks inside it were nearly empty after the last failed attempt to spray its enemies and its once wicked electro-coil trailed behind it, loose and ineffective.

From a dark corner across the cavern, Dr. Kaustik watched in horror as his SPIDER's existence came to an end. Sequoia smashed the Copterjet onto the doctor's beloved mechanical caretaker with brute force.

The slamming action ruptured its fuel tanks and caused an immense explosion that sent mighty Sequoia flying off his feet. Juniper and Mesquite lost their balance as well, while Cedar smartly ducked back into the tunnel he had just burrowed and Aspen veered clear from it all by flying outside the giant rip in the bay doors from where they had first entered.

The force of the blast caused a terrible trembling in the entire cavern. Rocks and beams started crashing to the ground. Smoke filled the air as the fire from the explosion burned wildly.

"Everyone out!" Mesquite yelled above the chaos. The rest of the Natural Forces hurried for the opening, dodging falling rocks and debris along the way. In seconds

they were all clear and safely outside.

Dr. Kaustik, clutching a portable breathing tank to his chest, retreated down one of the cave's passageways. A moment later, the entire cave collapsed — the mountain imploding on itself and burying everything inside under tons of Arizona limestone and sediment.

The Natural Forces team regrouped a few hundred yards away from the cavern and watched as it crumbled in on itself. Smoke from the fire and the dust billowed up into the evening air, blocking out the stars in the night sky. The ground was still rumbling and shuddering beneath their feet as if an earthquake was underway. After a few minutes it stopped completely, and the canyon was quiet again except for the sound of the rushing waters of the Colorado River.

By the next day, the animal younglings were miles away and seeking their next adventure. They knew a clue directing them would soon come their way, so they wandered about looking for food and staying out of trouble.

Sequoia's always sensitive nose led them to a dumpster behind a gas station up the road a ways and just off the interstate.

After gorging themselves on scraps from the garbage bin, they sat leisurely on a hill in some tall weeds and sagebrush under the shade of a disfigured pine tree. From a safe distance, they were watching humans scurry about the store. These people seemed to be constantly on the move, fueling their vehicles, buying snacks and visiting the restrooms. Even they seemed robot-like.

Mesquite broke the silence with a question, "Do you guys suppose they'll ever know how close they came to becoming victims of the very air they breathe?"

"I d-d-doubt it," Sequoia replied as he finished a half-eaten and slightly moldy bagel he had found in the

dumpster. "Maybe someday if they dig into that r-r-rubble and discover what's b-b-buried in there."

"I wonder how long they would have gotten away with it?" Juniper asked, speaking about the Axxes Conglomeration and their despicable plot. "What were they hoping to gain?"

Cedar grumbled the answer. "Money, I'm sure. With them, it's always about money."

"So, what's next?" Aspen asked.

"We wait," Mesquite said. "We relax and wait for a sign."

"That could take days...or weeks," she said impatiently. "It's hard enough being the only flyer in this group, but c'mon, the waiting is just killing me!"

"Hey, birdie, it's not like we all enjoy your company either," Cedar snapped. "Sometimes you just need to keep your beak..."

"Shh! Guys! Shut up!" Mesquite interrupted. "Look down there! It's a sign! It's our clue!"

At the gas station, a big truck had pulled up to refuel. It was towing a yacht behind it that was covered with a tight white canvas material for transporting it long distances.

"What are you t-t-talking about?" Sequoia asked. "It's just a pickup hauling a boat."

"Look closer, you dummy," Mesquite said. "What's

the name of the boat? Humans always name their boats."

The animals all leaned forward, focusing on the back of the boat. Painted there in fancy words was the boat's name: Journey North.

"It's a sign. We should go north!" Mesquite exclaimed.

"North?" Cedar said. "That's like forever from here!"

"Not if we hitch a ride! C'mon, the coast is clear!" Mesquite said excitedly and bolted out of the brush toward the filling station.

The other four looked at each other and sighed. Then they followed their buddy down to the boat loaded up on a heavy-duty trailer behind the big truck.

The man finished fueling his 4x4 and walked inside the store, leaving the area unsecured for five impulsive animal hitchhikers to easily access. They scrambled up into the back of the boat and hid under the bright white tarp that stretched over the top. It was nice inside – the yacht was certainly a very expensive one. It smelled of new leather, paint and plastics. The deck was made of real wood.

The critters all found comfortable spots and lay down to rest for a long journey ahead. In a few minutes, the driver of the truck came out of the store with a bagful of snacks and a super-sized soda in his hand. He hopped up in the cab of his truck and in seconds

they were out on the road, bound, unknowingly, for the state of Minnesota.

"Not bad, huh?" Mesquite quipped. "Hang with me and you travel in style!"

"Mesquite! Look out! Spider!" Cedar shouted.

The wolf pup screamed. His eyes popped wide open like saucers. He jumped up, hit his head on the tarp above and fell back down, landing on his stomach with his legs sprawled out. A pitiful "oomph" escaped from his mouth.

"Sorry, dude!" Cedar said as he burst out laughing. "It's just a daddy-longlegs!"

The whole gang, except for Mesquite who was embarrassingly trying to catch his breath, was cracking up and rolling about. They laughed so hard that tears came to their eyes.

"Very funny," Mesquite said. "Ha, ha. Very funny."

*****

Back in Los Angeles, Nathan Axxes was walking briskly down one of the highly polished, impeccably clean corridors. He was on his way to Dr. Kaustik's research and development lab. He was fuming.

Axxes flung open the heavy stainless-steel doors to the lab. "Kaustik!" he snapped.

The doctor stepped out from behind a large computer terminal. His arm was in a sling, bandages covered his head and face and he couldn't step with all his weight on his left foot. He was connected to a portable breathing tank that was on wheels. Several of them lined the far wall.

"Yes, sir," the doctor humbly replied.

Nathan glared at him, uncaring of his obvious injuries. "I read your report. And I have to say I find it awful hard to swallow," Axxes grumbled. "I'm glad to see you survived your little encounter, but do you realize how much you've cost me?"

The doctor spoke and for the first time Nathan noticed that one of the lenses of his glasses was cracked. "I do, sir, and I will make it up to you. I will find these creatures…"

Axxes interrupted him. "I don't really care about these creatures, Doctor. I'm out 1.5 billion dollars. I'm short forty, million-dollar Soldierjack workers and untold hours of manufacturing, design and investment. Just how do you suppose you're going to make that up?"

"Give me time to heal, Mr. Axxes," said the Mongolian physicist who was lucky to be alive. His voice was trembling a bit. "I will devise another way, another ingenious plan…"

Nathan had about all he could take and interrupted him again, "Enough already, you pathetic imbecile. You've been home more than a week now and you've not even left this lab – show me what you're working on."

The timid scientist led his boss over to the array of computer screens he was working on. Blueprints for a new machine were on display; most of them were 3-D images that rotated with schematics and mathematical formulas connected to them.

"What is this thing?" Axxes demanded. "It's the size of a tow-truck!"

"Oh, it's my latest creation, Mr. Axxes," Kaustik proudly replied. "I call it a Self-Controlled Onboard-Reactor-Powered Invincible Obedient Nexus. And you're going to like it, sir. You're going to like it a lot!"

COMING SOON!

The latest action-adventure chapter book in the all-new ongoing series starring the continent's most powerful animals!

Earth's greatest guardians clash with the world's most ruthless hunter when an undiscovered wildcat species gets in the way of buried nuclear weapons!

NATURAL FORCES™

Jinx of the Black Lynx

David Schmidt

HUNTER vs HUNTED

*It's predator against prey once Colonel Shaka sets his sights on the Natural Forces! Catch all the excitement in **Jinx of the Black Lynx!***

Brought together by the spirit of an ancient shaman, five rowdy animal orphans have been chosen to be protectors of the planet. Each creature - Wolf, Bear, Falcon, Ferret and Badger - was given the power to morph into their adult-warrior form, and each is endowed with amazing mystical weapons and superpowers!

Jinx of the Black Lynx...
The world's most lethal hunter, Colonel Shaka, is called in to hunt down and eradicate a newly discovered species of wild cat when its very existence threatens to uncover a secretly buried arsenal of nuclear weapons in northern Minnesota. Can the Natural Forces team save the last feline of its kind and survive themselves once Shaka and his brutal army of Soldierjacks target them as well?

Children's Fiction

$7.95

ISBN-13: 978-1-934980-29-3
ISBN-10: 1-934980-29-3

5 0795

www.cablepublishing.com

DAVID A. SCHMIDT
Artist & Author

BIO

Born and raised in rural Wisconsin, David Schmidt has always has an aptitude for artistic endeavors. Upon graduating with honors from high school, Schmidt moved to Colorado and joined the National Guard as a means to pursue an art degree.

After returning home from a deployment with his unit for Operation Desert Shield/Desert Storm in 1991, Schmidt worked for a Denver-based children's book fair company. It was in those elementary schools and working with the kids, teachers and parents that he found himself drawn to creating his own children's books.

Meanwhile, Schmidt moved into a position for the Colorado National Guard as an illustrator, then military journalist and, finally, as historian. These occupations honed his skills and guided him further down his path toward publishing.

David Schmidt resides in Lone Tree, Colorado, with his wife and is the owner of Media Uprising - a creative company that serves as the outlet for his diverse talents. He holds a degree in Interactive Media Design from the Art Institute of Pittsburgh.

What Does a Detective Do?

by Juan Lester
illustrated by Donna Catanese

Editorial Offices: Glenview, Illinois • Parsippany, New Jersey • New York, New York
Sales Offices: Needham, Massachusetts • Duluth, Georgia • Glenview, Illinois
Coppell, Texas • Ontario, California • Mesa, Arizona